Amir thrust aside the heavy curtain.

No sign of the girl.

He checked, senses suddenly alert, his nape prickling.

An instant later he threw up a blocking arm as someone leapt at him out of the gloom. A jingle of clashing coins at her belt warned him of her identity just in time.

Instinct saved him. Instinct honed by years perfecting a warrior's skills and others learning less honourable ways to survive. He pivoted and snapped an arm around her wrist, just as a blade pricked the base of his neck.

'Wild cat!'

Annie West spent her childhood with her nose between the covers of a book—a habit she retains. After years preparing government reports and official correspondence she decided to write something she *really* enjoys. And there's nothing she loves more than a great romance. Despite her office-bound past she has managed a few interesting moments—including a marriage offer with the promise of a herd of camels to sweeten the contract. She is happily married to her ever-patient husband (who has never owned a dromedary). They live with their two children amongst the tall eucalypts at beautiful Lake Macquarie, on Australia's east coast. You can e-mail Annie at www.annie-west.com, or write to her at PO Box 1041, Warners Bay, NSW 2282, Australia.

Recent titles by the same author:

PASSION, PURITY AND THE PRINCE
PRINCE OF SCANDAL

GIRL IN THE BEDOUIN TENT

BY
ANNIE WEST

MILLS &
BOON

All the characters in this book have no existence outside the imagination of the author, and have no relation whatsoever to anyone bearing the same name or names. They are not even distantly inspired by any individual known or unknown to the author, and all the incidents are pure invention.

First published in Great Britain 2011
by Mills & Boon, an imprint of Harlequin (UK) Limited,
Eton House, 18-24 Paradise Road, Richmond, Surrey TW9 1SR

© Annie West 2011

ISBN: 978 0 263 88690 0

Harlequin (UK) policy is to use papers that are natural, renewable and recyclable products and made from wood grown in sustainable forests. The logging and manufacturing process conform to the legal environmental regulations of the country of origin.

Printed and bound in Spain
by Blackprint CPI, Barcelona

GIRL IN THE BEDOUIN TENT

With thanks and love to Andrew,
who has been an inspiration.
What a guy!

CHAPTER ONE

GRAVEL crunched under Amir's boots as he strode across the starlit compound to the tent provided for him. It had been a tedious evening in poor company. Playing guest to the renegade tribal leader in a neighbouring state was *not* how Amir chose to spend his time. Especially since he had important personal business to conclude when he returned to his own country.

'Highness.' Faruq hurried after him. 'We need to consult before the negotiations begin.'

'No.' Amir shook his head. 'Get your sleep. Tomorrow will be a long day.' Especially for Faruq. Amir's aide was city-bred, not used to this wild, remote region, where old ways held sway and diplomacy was rough and ready.

'But Highness...' The protest died as Amir gestured to Mustafa's guards stationed around the tent. Ostensibly for Amir's protection, but undoubtedly to spy if possible.

Faruq ducked his head, then murmured, 'There's also the girl.'

The girl.

Amir's pace slowed as he recalled the woman Mustafa had given him tonight with such ostentation. Blonde hair that shimmered in the lamplight like fluid silk framing a pale face. Luminous violet eyes that stared boldly back, holding Amir's gaze in a way few men and no women in this region of traditional values would dare.

The unexpected combination of beauty and defiance had for an instant stalled the air in his lungs.

Until he'd remembered his taste ran to sophisticated women. Not dancing girls, or whores in gaudy make-up presented by their master to pleasure a visiting dignitary.

Amir had his pick of gorgeous women on six continents. He chose his own bed partners.

And yet…something about her had snared his interest. Perhaps the haughty way she'd arched her delicate blonde eyebrows in a look that would have done an empress proud.

Fleetingly that had intrigued.

'You doubt my capacity to handle her?'

Faruq smothered a chuckle. 'Of course not, Sire. But there's something…unusual there.'

Unusual was right. In Monte Carlo, Moscow or Stockholm her colouring wouldn't warrant a second glance. As for those eyes—that particular shade surely indicated the use of coloured contact lenses. But here, in rough border country inhabited by nomads, brigands and subsistence farmers?

'Don't concern yourself, Faruq. I'm sure she and I will come to some…accommodation.'

Amir nodded dismissal and entered the tent. He removed his boots in the small anteroom, his feet sinking into layered carpets.

Would she be on the bed waiting for him, her skirts spread about her? Or perhaps she'd be naked. No doubt she'd offer herself with the finesse of a professional.

Despite his distaste, Amir's pulse hummed at the memory of a lush, sultry mouth at odds with the fire in her blazing eyes. That mouth promised sensual pleasure enough to interest any man.

Amir thrust aside the heavy curtain.

One step in and he registered the dimmed lamp on the far side of the room.

No sign of the girl.

He checked, senses suddenly alert, his nape prickling.

An instant later he threw up a blocking arm as someone

leapt at him out of the gloom. Something heavy hit him a glancing blow and he swung round, grabbing his assailant.

He caught at a voluminous cloak that fell as he clutched it. A jingle of clashing coins at her belt warned him of her identity just in time. He pulled back sharply to avoid felling her with a single knockout blow.

Amir caught her arm and twisted it behind her back. His movements were controlled, precise, despite the way she threshed and fought. He'd learned to wrestle with full-grown heavyweights. He couldn't use those tactics on a woman, even a woman who ambushed him in his own chamber.

Still she fought. She was like a tigress, alternately trying to wrest herself free or disable him with vicious kicks to the groin.

'Enough!' His patience was at an end. He reached to grab her free arm. But before he could catch it she twisted, rose and brought her arm down in a desperate slashing motion.

Instinct saved him. Instinct honed by years perfecting a warrior's skills and others learning less honourable ways to survive. He pivoted and snapped an arm around her wrist, just as a blade pricked the base of his neck.

'Wild cat!' He squeezed and the knife clattered to the floor. Without compunction he hooked his foot around her legs and brought her down, slamming into her as she collapsed. She landed heavily on her back, his full weight on her, his legs surrounding hers.

An instant later he'd captured both her slender wrists and pinioned them on the carpet high above her head.

She was spent, so still that for a moment he even wondered if she breathed. Then he felt the tremulous rise of full breasts beneath him and heard a raw, shuddering gasp as she drew in air.

Slowly he raised his hand to his throat. A thin trail of wetness slid down from his collarbone.

She'd stabbed him!

Reflexively his hold on her hands tightened and she cried

out—a sharp mew of pain, quickly stifled. Immediately he eased his grip.

Jaw set, he reached for the blade on the floor. Her breath hitched and she froze rigid, but he barely noticed as he balanced it in his hand. Small, sharp and beautiful. An antique paring knife. Keen enough to peel fruit, or inflict serious injury on the unwary.

The blade caught the lamplight and she flinched. What? Did she think he'd use it on her?

With a curse he tossed it to the far side of the room.

'Who sent you to do this? Mustafa?'

It didn't make sense. His host had no reason to wish him dead. Nor could he think of anyone who'd resort to royal assassination. Yet the trickle of blood across his skin was real.

This was one hell of a way to spice up a distasteful duty visit!

Curiosity and fury vied for dominance as he surveyed those lush, scarlet lips now parted to drag in air. The impossibly violet kohl-rimmed eyes, huge beneath thick purple eyeshadow.

'Who *are* you?' He leaned over her, his face bare inches from hers, but her expression was blank, as if schooled to show no fear no matter the threat.

Cursing, he rose on one arm. The movement pressed his groin harder against her body and part of his brain registered her satisfying softness, an innate invitation he couldn't quite ignore despite his scorching anger.

He forced his mind into action. This was no time to be distracted.

If she had one knife there might be others. He rolled to one side, careful to keep her thighs pinioned with one of his and her hands imprisoned.

Her breathing shallowed as he surveyed the expanse of bare skin revealed by her belly dancer's outfit. Her breasts rose and fell rapidly, threatening to pull free of the skimpy bodice. Surely there was no room for a lethal weapon there.

His gaze dropped, skimming her smooth, pale torso, past the dip to her neat waist accentuated by a decorative chain and the flare of her hips. The old-fashioned coin belt sitting low on her hips might be wide enough to conceal something, but her side-slit skirt was too filmy for a hiding place.

Amir lowered his palm to her belly, registering the flinch of her velvet soft skin. He paused. In all his years he'd never touched an unwilling woman. His mouth flattened in distaste. This had to be done—it wasn't sexual, just self-preservation.

Deftly he slid his hand under her belt.

Instantly she erupted in convulsing movement. Her hips bucked and writhed, her torso twisted, her legs scrabbled fruitlessly for purchase.

'No! Please, no!' The words rang hoarsely. Not in any of the local dialects but in a language rarely heard here.

'You're English?'

Amir whipped his head round and froze as he saw the expression in those wide violet eyes.

Sheer terror.

It was his stillness that finally penetrated Cassie's panic. That and the fact he'd slipped his large hand free of her clothes and held it, palm outward, as if to placate her.

Her heart thudded high in her throat and clammy sweat beaded her brow as she stared up at him. She couldn't get her breath, though she gulped in huge, racking breaths.

'You're English?' he said again in that language, and his black eyebrows drew down in a scowl that accentuated the hard, sculpted lines of his face. He looked fierce and frightening and aggressively male.

Would it matter if she was English? Frantically her mind scrabbled to work out if her nationality would make a difference. Was one nationality safer than another in this place where travellers were abducted and imprisoned?

'American?' His head tilted to one side and tiny lines of concentration wrinkled his brow.

He didn't look angry now, but the weight of his solid thigh, the firm grasp that bound her wrists, reminded her she was still at his mercy. He could subdue her with ease.

Her eyes flicked to the scarlet dribble of blood at his throat and she shuddered, fear rising anew. She'd thought to save herself with a pre-emptive attack, knocking him out with the brass pot, but he'd been too quick for her. Too quick, too strong, too dangerous.

'Please.' It was a hoarse whisper from a throat tight with dread. 'Don't do this.'

Every muscle and tendon in her body tensed as she waited for his response.

His sensual mouth lifted at one corner in a snarl of displeasure and his eyebrows shot up. 'You want me to release you? After this?' He gestured to his wound.

Cassie let go a quivering breath. His deep voice with its crisp English and just a hint of an exotic accent had broached her defences. And sharpened the nightmare horror of her situation.

This couldn't be happening. It just couldn't!

'I'm sorry,' she said. 'I just…' Her eyelids fluttered as the world began to dip and swirl about her.

Desperately she clawed back to full consciousness. Fear and fury had kept her strong through the last twenty-four hours. She refused to faint now! Not when she sensed she'd be safe only as long as she kept him talking.

Cassie snapped her eyes open to find he'd bent closer. She saw the slight shadow darkening his strong jaw, a pale scar to the side of his mouth, the way his nostrils flared as if scenting her. The gleam of eyes so dark and so close they looked black and fathomless.

'Please,' she choked. 'Don't rape me.'

Instantly he reared back, letting cool air rush between them. His eyes widened and his fingers tightened convulsively around her wrists. She bit her tongue rather than cry out her pain.

'You think…?' He gestured to her skirts with his free hand and suddenly it was distaste she read in his expression. 'You *really* think…?' He shook his head slowly and said something under his breath in Arabic.

She flinched at the violence in his tone but refused to look away. She was already at his mercy. To appear weak could be a fatal mistake.

His mouth snapped shut, his eyes zeroing in on her face. She felt the intensity of his stare like the burn of ice on bare flesh.

He drew a breath that expanded his chest impressively. Sickly she realised she had no hope if he forced her.

Memories swirled. The metallic tang of terror filled her mouth again as she recalled being pinioned against a door by a man twice her size and three times her age. She'd been only sixteen, but even now she remembered the feel of his meaty hand thrusting inside her shirt, his other hand bruising her thigh, his weight suffocating as he tried to—

'I would not stoop to such an act. No matter what the provocation.' The stranger's voice rang clear with outrage, shattering the past.

Cassie blinked up at a face carved of stone. His jaw clenched as if she'd offered him the worst imaginable insult and he tilted his head, looking down at her as if he'd never seen her like.

'I prefer my women willing.'

His headscarf had come off in the tussle. Glossy black hair was cut close to his well-shaped head. His eyes flashed and emotion drew the skin tight over an impressive bone structure for which any of the leading men she'd performed with would give their eye teeth.

This man would have no trouble finding willing women.

'Then let me go.'

Lying half-naked beneath him, she couldn't trust his word no matter how indignant he looked. She was too aware of his big, hard body, all heavy muscle and bone, imprisoning her. Of his callused hand encircling hers with almost casual dominance. Of the intrinsically male scent of his skin in her nostrils.

'When I'm sure you're not hiding another weapon.'

Cassie's eyes bulged. That was what he'd been doing? Looking for concealed weapons? If she'd had something other than that little knife they'd left beside the fruit platter she'd have used it as soon as he walked through the door. When she'd felt his hand thrusting down into her skirt she'd been sure—

She choked as a bubble of desperate mirth rose from tight lungs. She tried to force it away but the idea was ludicrous. As if there was space in her skimpy clothes to hide anything! Her vision blurred as she gasped for breath over the ragged, sickening laughter she couldn't stifle.

'Stop it! Now!' Firm hands shook her shoulders.

The off-key laughter died abruptly.

He sat on his heels, his eyes fixed on her. This close they looked like black velvet. His skin was golden, his brows dark as sin. A hard angular jaw and strong nose gave him an air of purpose.

His big hands clasped her shoulders, a reminder of his latent strength. A wisp of something shimmered in the air between them for a second. Something new. Her dazed brain tried to grab at it but it vanished as he withdrew his hands and she drew another breath, less ragged this time.

Her wrists throbbed as blood surged through them again. Slowly, each movement painful, she dragged her hands down to cradle them at her chest.

He'd let her go! She could scarcely believe it.

'Thank you,' she whispered, swallowing hard.

Yet, free of his hold, exhaustion engulfed her as the manic surge of adrenalin ebbed.

Twenty-four hours living on the edge of terror had sapped her reserves of strength. It took a few moments to gather herself and find the energy to stir.

Conscious of his gaze assessing every movement, of his tense body still far too close, she rolled to her side and braced her hands against the carpet, ready to get up. Each action took so much energy, and she still felt winded from the impact of what surely must be six feet three of powerfully muscled man tumbling her to the floor.

'What's that?' His voice was sharp.

Cassie looked over her shoulder, eyes wide.

'What?'

'On your back.' He gestured towards her bare back but thankfully didn't touch. 'Down low, just above your skirt, and there, on your thigh.'

Cassie's lips compressed as she pushed herself to her knees.

'Bruises, I expect. The guard likes to exert his authority.' Her lips twisted as she remembered the sadistic glitter in the big man's eyes as he'd laid into her. She'd made the error of defying him. How soon would she have to return to face his tender mercies?

Another burst of Arabic sounded and she swung her head around.

The expression in those dark eyes was ugly.

Instinctively she raised clenched hands in defensive fists.

'Don't look at me like that!' If anything, he scowled more ferociously. Finally he breathed deep, as if searching for calm. 'You have nothing to fear from me.'

It took a moment to realise his gaze had moved to the chain circling her waist and the longer, heavier one connected to it. The one that tethered her to the wide bed on one side of the room.

Cassie had spent fruitless hours trying desperately to prise one of the links open. But nothing had worked, not even the knife. Her fingers were raw and her nails torn from the attempt.

Heat surged into her cheeks as she followed his stare. The symbolism of that chain, securing her like a slave to the bed, was too blatant to be missed.

She was here for his pleasure, to service his needs. As she watched expressions flit across his stark features, Cassie was sure she spied fleeting masculine speculation there.

Defiance flared in her belly.

Cassie knew the brutal power imbalance between a man and a woman kept solely for his amusement. Even if her own society dressed it up as something a little less blatant, it was a role she'd vowed long ago to avoid. Given her background, the thought of being any man's sexual plaything made her break out in a sweat.

It was an appalling cosmic joke that she of all people should find herself in this situation!

'Where's the key?'

Cassie lifted her chin. She injected insouciance into her tone to counteract the ridiculous shame she felt. As if she'd had a say in this! 'If I knew *that* I wouldn't still be here.'

Silently he surveyed her, his skimming glance making her hyperaware of every bare inch of skin and of the weight of encircling metal at her waist.

He sprang to his feet and retrieved her cloak from the floor.

'Here. Cover yourself.' The order was brusque, as if the sight of her offended him.

Looking up at his spare, powerful face, half averted, Cassie wondered if it were true. That he wasn't interested in…

'Thank you.' The words were muffled as she snatched the material and dragged it close. Its scratchy warmth settled around her but didn't counteract the cold welling inside. Suddenly her skin was covered in goosebumps and her teeth chattered. She slumped back on her heels, wrapping her arms around herself for warmth. The mountain air was cold at night, but Cassie knew it was shock finally taking its toll.

She watched him busy himself lighting another lamp and the brazier. The warm glow and cheering crackle of the fire reached her, yet still she felt frozen.

'Come. There's food. You'll feel better after you've eaten.'

'I won't feel better till I'm out of here!'

She glared up, all her resentment focusing on the man towering above her: tall, dark and far more compelling than mere handsome could ever be.

How could she notice that at a time like this?

Was shock affecting her ability to think?

He paced forward, extending a hand, and a tremor rippled through her at the thought of touching him again. His powerful body was still imprinted on hers.

Instinct shrieked that touching him was dangerous.

Cassie pretended not to notice his gesture and scrambled up, feeling the worse for wear. Acting kept her fit and agile, but being crash-tackled to the floor by a man with the hard body of an athlete was not something she trained for.

Breathlessly she stood, swaying only a little, determined not to reach for support.

If possible, his expression hardened even more, his jaw set like stone.

'Who are you?' Her voice emerged strident and challenging.

'My name is Amir ibn Masud Al Jaber.'

He inclined his head in a smooth gesture of introduction and waited, as if expecting a reaction.

'I know your name.' Cassie made a frustrated gesture, trying to remember how she knew his name. She'd never seen him before. That face, that presence was unforgettable.

'I am Sheikh of Tarakhar.'

'Sheikh? Do you mean…?' No, it was preposterous.

'Leader, in your language.'

Cassie's eyes bulged. No wonder she'd known his name! The Sheikh of Tarakhar was renowned for his fabulous wealth and for the absolute power he wielded within his kingdom.

It was his country she'd travelled through yesterday.

Why was he here? Was he in league with the men who'd done this to her?

Fear crowded close again. Cassie wrapped her arms tighter round her torso and began to sidle out of reach.

'And you are?' He didn't move but his deep voice stopped her in her tracks. She braced herself to meet his gleaming gaze.

'My name is Cassandra Denison. Cassie.'

'Cassandra.' The familiar syllables joined in an unfamiliar, exotic curl of sound. She told herself it was his hint of an accent that made her name sound different, so seductive.

She swayed a little—or was that the flickering light?

'Come! You need sustenance.' He didn't quite click his fingers, but his abrupt gesture made her step automatically towards a low, brass-topped table.

Her instant response to his command infuriated her, but she had more important things on her mind. Cassie's eyes rounded. The knife was back where she'd found it, beside a platter of fruit and almonds.

He trusted her with the blade? Or was it a trick to lull her into relaxing?

She eyed the entrance to the vast room, the heavy material that blocked the cool night air. Were the guards still on duty around the tent, making it impossible to escape even if she could break the barbaric chain that marked her as his possession?

A hand closed around her elbow and she jumped, alarm skittering through her. She whipped round to find impenetrable dark eyes fixed on her. His scowl had gone. In its place something like sympathy softened his features.

'You cannot run. Mustafa's guards would seize you before you got ten metres. Besides, you'd stand no chance alone in the mountains, especially at night.'

Cassie sucked in a desperate breath. Were her thoughts so obvious? She tilted her chin. 'Mustafa?'

'Our host. The man who presented you to me.'

Holding her arm, he half pushed, half supported her till her legs gave way and she plopped onto a pile of cushions. Instantly he released her.

A moment later, with an easy grace that held her unwilling gaze, he sank to face her across the low table.

Even seated he loomed too big for comfort. He crowded her space, dominating her senses. Cassie registered his scent: sandalwood and spicy male. Her nostrils flared and reaction feathered through her, jangling her nerves with something other than alarm. She sat straighter, making herself meet his gaze head on.

The flickering light of the brazier accentuated the strong lines of his face. A face that surely belonged in a storybook tale of Arabian nights and proud princes.

His deep voice broke across her hectic thoughts.

'Now, Cassandra Denison, you can explain what's going on.'

CHAPTER TWO

CASSIE'S eyes flicked from his flattened mouth to the tiny trickle of blood drying on the burnished skin of his neck. She drew a slow breath as he picked up the paring knife, but relaxed with a shiver of relief when he merely wiped it clean on a snowy cloth and began to pare an orange. Mesmerised, she watched the precise way he sliced the peel, the supple flick of strong wrists and the deft movements of his long fingers.

'I'm not accustomed to waiting.' Steel threaded his smooth voice and she started.

'And I'm not accustomed to being abducted!'

Straight black brows winged up. 'Abduction? That changes things.' He stilled, his eyes on her.

Cassie had the feeling he saw deep, beyond the overdone make-up, the decorative henna on her hands and feet and the dark cloak. That he saw right down to the woman trying desperately to conquer fear with bravado.

The silence lengthened. She should be pleading, demanding help. Persuading him with her eloquence. Words were her stock in trade, after all. Yet something in his steady, assessing gaze dried the words on her tongue. Her agitated pulse slowed a fraction.

When at last he spoke again his tone was light. 'You must forgive my curiosity. Being attacked with a knife is something of a novelty. It makes me inquisitive.'

His lips quirked up at one side and Cassie's heart gave a tiny jump of surprise.

She wanted to trust him, but could she?

Was he in cahoots with her abductors?

'You mean the chain didn't give it away? The fact that I might be here against my will?' Cassie lifted her chin. If only anger could melt the hard metal that kept her captive!

'I'm afraid I had other things on my mind.'

She felt an unwilling flicker of appreciation at his self-deprecating humour. He was a cool customer. Being attacked by a desperate woman wielding a knife hadn't ruffled his composure one iota!

Nor had it affected his exquisite manners. With another graceful movement he reached for a ewer and bowl and silently invited her to wash her hands. Despite her dire situation, or perhaps because of it, his old-fashioned courtesy soothed her shredded nerves.

Slowly Cassie extended her hands over the bowl. He poured water over her fingers, waited till she rubbed them clean, then poured again.

He passed her a towel of fine cotton, careful not to touch her. Cassie drew in a quick breath of relief and dried her hands, trying not to notice that even his hands were attractive—strong and well shaped.

Instead she concentrated on the soft comfort of the towel. How different the luxury here compared with the Spartan tent where she'd been held!

Only the best for a royal sheikh.

'Besides,' he continued as if uninterrupted, 'the chain could have been a ploy.'

'A ploy?' Cassie's voice rose and her body froze in outrage. 'A ploy? You think I'm wearing this thing for *fun*? It's heavy and uncomfortable and…inhuman!'

And it made her feel like a chattel, a *thing* rather than a person.

Cassie pulled the thick cloak tighter round herself, seeking comfort in its concealing folds.

The abduction had been shocking and terrifying, but being

tethered with a chain like an animal plumbed the depths of her darkest fears. It put her captors' intentions on a new and horrible level.

Even her mother, whose life had revolved around pleasing a man, had never faced a reality so brutal.

'As you say. Even in this lawless part of the world, I didn't expect to find kidnap and slavery.'

At her wide-eyed stare he went on. 'In the old days, centuries ago, slaves were held that way.' He nodded curtly to the chain that snaked across the floor towards the bed. 'It's a slave chain. I thought it possible Mustafa had used it symbolically, rather than seriously.'

'You thought I might have *agreed* to this? That I *chose* to dress this way?' Cassie snapped her mouth shut, remembering her struggles as the women had stripped her clothes away. The horror when they'd produced this gaudy outfit that barely covered her breasts and drew attention to every curve.

She remembered too the searing look, quickly veiled, in this man's eyes when she'd been brought before him in the communal tent. It had heated her as no fire could.

'I didn't know what to think. I don't know you.'

Cassie drew a calming breath. Finally she nodded.

He was right. He knew as little of her as she did of him. The chain *could* have been a stage prop worn for effect—there to spice the jaded appetites of a man who got turned on by the idea of a woman totally at his mercy. A woman with no function but to please him.

Was Amir that sort of man?

Without warning that ancient memory broke through her weary brain's defences again. The one memory she usually kept locked tightly away. Of Curtis Bevan, who'd been her mother's lover the year Cassie turned sixteen. How he'd strutted around her mother's apartment with condescending pride, knowing everything there was bought with his money. Even his lover. How he'd turned his proprietorial eyes on Cassie that day she'd come home for Christmas—

'Cassie?'

The sound of her name in that soft-as-suede voice shattered the recollection. She looked up into a cool obsidian gaze that she would swear saw too much. Her breath snared and for a moment she foundered, caught between her nightmare past and the present.

Deliberately she straightened her shoulders.

'For the record, I don't want to be here! When you came in I thought…' Her words dried at the recollection of what she'd thought. That he'd come here for sex. That it wouldn't matter if she was unwilling.

'You thought you had no choice.' His voice was low and his expression softened. 'The pre-emptive strike was a good move. A brave one.'

Cassie shook her head. 'Just desperate.'

It had become clear within seconds she had no chance against him. He'd subdued her so quickly, lashed her threshing limbs into immobility and toppled her with an ease that merely reinforced his physical superiority.

Whatever happened now she had more sense than to try to overcome this man physically. She needed him fighting for her, not against her.

'Who is this Mustafa? What makes him think he has the right to give me to you like this?'

Amir shrugged, his wide shoulders drawing her unwilling gaze. She told herself her fascination with his sculpted features, his aura of power, was because he was her only hope of getting out of here.

'Mustafa is a bandit chief. He rules these mountains down to the border with Tarakhar. We're in his camp.'

Silently he offered her a plate of orange segments and dates. It was her first food in over twenty-four hours.

Yet she hesitated, wondering at the possibility it had been tampered with. That fear had kept her from devouring it earlier while she waited alone, frantically trying to break the chain.

But he had no need to drug her. She was already at his mercy.

Determined, Cassie forced her mind from the insidious thought.

Carefully she reached for a piece of orange. Its flavour burst like sunshine in her mouth, stinging like blazes where she'd bitten her tongue during their skirmish. Her eyes almost closed in sheer bliss despite the pain. She swallowed and reached for another piece.

'You were going to tell me how you got here.' The dark voice jerked her attention back to the man seated opposite her.

His hooded eyes gleamed with an expression she couldn't name. Was it curiosity, as he'd said? Had she imagined that flash of predatory male interest when he'd first seen her and again as she lay beneath him?

Cassie recalled his touch on her bare skin and shivered. Anxiety swirled in her stomach, and a flutter of something else she couldn't put a name to.

'I was travelling through Tarakhar by bus.'

'By yourself?' Was that disapproval in his tone?

Cassie's spine stiffened. 'I'm twenty-three and more than capable of travelling alone!'

Circumstances had forced Cassie into independence early. She'd never had the luxury of relying on others. Besides, her destination—a rural town near the border—wasn't on the tourist route. She'd had to travel overland for the last part of the journey.

'Visitors are welcomed and treated with respect in Tarakhar. Yet it's advisable not to travel alone.'

'So I've discovered.' Cassie shot him an eloquent look, her ire rising. Anger, she'd found, was preferable to fear. How dared he blame her for what had happened? She was the innocent party!

'A travel warning for foreign visitors might be useful. Perhaps you could have one issued since you're in charge?' Her voice dropped to saccharine sweetness. 'Maybe something about travellers being fair game for kidnappers?'

His eyes narrowed, yet she couldn't read his expression.

Finally he nodded. 'You're right. Action must be taken.'

Cassie watched the grooves deepen around his mouth and wondered what action he had in mind. Despite his stillness and his relaxed pose, she sensed he wasn't nearly as laid-back as he appeared.

Finally she asked the question she'd been putting off. 'You said Mustafa rules these mountains.' She paused, delaying the inevitable. 'Aren't we in Tarakhar any more?'

'No. We're no longer in my country but in the neighbouring state of Bhutran. It's Mustafa's tribal territory and he rules with an iron fist.'

Cassie's heart plunged. She'd already experienced the iron fist. But she'd hoped, prayed, they were still in Tarakhar, where help might reach her. Where Sheikh Amir had authority. Bhutran was a lawless state—notoriously so.

Despair threatened to swamp her but she fought it. Her only hope lay in not giving up. She still had to find a way out of here.

Cassie forced herself to reach for the fruit platter. She needed energy to escape.

Amir watched her devour the fruit with delicate greed. The combination of feisty opponent, all flashing eyes and quick tongue, with soft femininity intrigued him. More than he could remember being intrigued in a long, long time.

In repose her lips were a soft pout of invitation, glistening with fruit juice. The tip of her pink tongue appeared now and then to swipe the excess moisture. Amir realised her sensuality was innate, not contrived.

Yet it wasn't anything as simple as sexual magnetism alone that intrigued him.

The moment Mustafa had presented her in a flourish of generosity her sparking gaze had sizzled across the space between them, piercing Amir's boredom at the gathering's false bonhomie and crude revelry.

Later, through his fury at her attack, he'd still registered her pliant body cushioning him and her delicate scent: desert rose and warm woman.

He'd known women, *had* women in all sorts of circumstances. It had become rare for one to quicken his pulse.

She reached for a date and her cloak slipped enough to reveal the smooth, pale skin of her collarbone, her cleavage. The cloak slid again to show straining midnight blue silk. The material scooped indecently low, revealing far too much of one full, perfect breast.

He recalled how she'd looked in the skimpy dancing costume. She was all lush curves, with a slender waist accentuated by what he'd thought at the time was merely a decorative chain.

Amir yanked his gaze away. He needed to focus!

'Why were you travelling in this region?' The border country wasn't a sightseeing area.

Violet eyes clashed with his before she looked away, hurriedly securing the gaping front of her cloak.

'I've been accepted on to a volunteer programme, teaching English to adults for a couple of months.'

'You're a teacher?' He tried not to let his surprise show. Obviously these weren't her normal clothes. Look at the way she'd just covered up. Yet still he found it difficult, imagining her in a classroom.

'It's not my field back home in Australia, but they were eager for volunteers and it sounded…fulfilling.'

This woman grew more interesting by the moment. He could picture her at home in a bustling, lively city. She was so full of energy and opinions. Teaching in a provincial school was the last place he'd imagine her. 'How did you get here?'

One neat hand clutched the coarse fabric of her cloak and her jaw hardened.

'The bus broke down in the foothills near the border.

Apparently it was a major mechanical problem, something that couldn't be fixed quickly. All the passengers headed off across country to their own homes. There was just me and the driver left, and then…' She shrugged, a jerky little movement that belied her show of casualness. 'Then we heard a sound like thunder.'

She flashed a look at him. Behind the defiance he detected a shadow that might have been fear.

Instinctively Amir leaned towards her, only to straighten abruptly when she recoiled.

It wasn't a reaction to which he was accustomed.

'Horsemen came galloping down from the mountains. They grabbed me.' Her voice flattened to an emotionless pitch that anyone less observant might mistake for insouciance. 'I lost sight of the driver in all the dust and milling horses.' She paused. 'He'd been kind to me. I…don't know what happened to him.'

'You needn't fear for him. A report of the raid came through as I travelled here. The driver is recovering from concussion in hospital.'

Anger ignited in Amir's belly. For Mustafa to have led a violent raid and the abduction of a foreign national inside Tarakhan's borders the day before Amir's visit was little short of a direct insult.

Yet it wasn't Mustafa's arrogance that rankled. It was what had been done to this remarkable woman. Terrified, abducted and abused, she still managed to hold her own, challenging him and giving no ground even when it was patently clear she was dependent on his goodwill.

Was it her vulnerability or her courage that sliced straight through the diffidence he wore like a second skin?

Long dormant emotions stirred uneasily.

It was understandable he'd feel pity. Yet when had he truly cared on a personal level about anyone? Cared for anything but work or his own pleasure?

His lips twisted. *He hadn't.*

Amir was self-sufficient and glad of it. He'd never experienced love, even as a child. Nor had friendship been permitted with the other boys who, with him, had learned the ways of a Tarakhan warrior under his uncle's stern eye.

With the ease of long practice Amir turned his mind to more important matters.

Tonight he'd been the polite guest, playing the game of diplomacy and courtesy to the hilt. He'd allowed Mustafa to bask in the honour of hosting a man far more powerful than he could ever hope to be. Tomorrow his host would find a change in his revered guest.

Mustafa might live in a chaotic nation where the rule of law barely existed, but he'd soon discover the Sheikh of Tarakhar was no pushover. Earlier Amir had been impatient at the need for slow negotiations when an all-important personal arrangement required his attention at home. Now he looked forward to making Mustafa squirm.

'The driver's really OK?'

Amir saw concern on her pale features and felt a stab of admiration. Despite her own situation she was worried for the driver.

'He'll be fine. He was knocked unconscious, which would be why he didn't raise the alarm about your kidnap.'

A tide of impatience rose that he was sitting talking when every nerve screamed for action. Amir was about to surge to his feet when her expression caught his notice.

She pretended strength and insouciance, yet her posture was a little too perfect. Instead of lounging on the comfortable cushions she sat erect, as if ready for anything, even sudden attack. She'd flinched earlier at his exclamations of outrage. Obviously she still didn't trust him. How could she?

Amir subsided onto the banked cushions.

'You've been with Mustafa's men since the abduction?'

She nodded slowly, and he couldn't help but read significance into the fact that this time she didn't elaborate. He'd already learned she wasn't afraid to express her opinion.

What had they done to her?

His stomach clenched at the possibilities.

Cassie watched him pour juice into a chased goblet that looked as if it dated from the time of the crusades. Who knew? Perhaps it did.

His hand, the colour of dark honey, looked strong and capable as he held it out to her.

'Thank you.' She reached to take it from him, careful only to touch the cool metal. She remembered the heat of his skin on hers, the curious sensation when he touched her, and knew better than to risk further contact.

He was too disturbing, even now when he sat with easy composure, drawing out her story, each movement measured and non-threatening. She couldn't forget her sense of peril as she'd stared into fathomless dark eyes and that grim slash of a mouth.

What disturbed her most was the conviction the danger lay not only in his physical strength, his ability to subdue her bodily. It lay in that indefinable aura that tugged at her consciousness. The way her senses, though battered by kidnap and confinement, stirred when he gave that rueful half smile. When he apologised for being distracted, fighting for his life. When his eyes met hers and something unnamed sizzled through the air.

That didn't stop her covertly noticing the slight shadow along his jaw that made him look like a sexy bandit, and the way his full lower lip and mobile mouth turned severe features into something far too appealing.

Cassie blinked, shocked. Her mind was wandering. She clasped her hands tight and leaned closer.

'Now you know I'm here against my will, you'll be able to get me away from here.' Even outside his realm surely he'd be able to help her.

The silence lengthened. Her confident smile grew ragged.

The hastily stitched fabric of her defences began to unravel.

Each second that ticked past shredded her nerves. The thud of her heart, so fast she felt dizzy with it, almost deafened her.

He *must* help!

He couldn't *ignore* what had happened to her.

Finally he spoke. 'Unfortunately it's not that simple.'

'Not simple?' Her stunned voice echoed hoarsely. She felt betrayed. She'd counted on his assistance.

'I'm afraid not. You need to be patient.'

Stiffening her spine, Cassie stared at the man sitting so imperturbably. Shadows from the lamps cast elongated shadows across the strong lines of his face, accentuating the way his hooded eyelids veiled his expression.

Didn't he understand her desperation?

Unless he'd decided it was in his own interests not to help her.

Had she been gulled into a false sense of security by his calm questions and his mellow tone?

Breathing slowly, trying not to hyperventilate, Cassie told herself the Sheikh of Tarakhar couldn't be interested in her. She had none of the sultry allure or seductive experience she imagined his lovers possessed. Despite the stark austerity of his clothes, he looked like a man who'd only settle for the best.

If it came to sexual skills, Cassie wasn't in the running.

But then experience wasn't always required. She knew that from bitter experience.

Surreptitiously she slid her hand under cover of her cloak to where he had carelessly abandoned the knife, holding his gaze unblinking all the while.

'Sheathe your claws, kitten. You have no need of a blade now.'

Kitten! Indignation swamped doubt as her fingers clenched convulsively on the hilt of the fruit knife.

'No?' She tilted her chin.

'No. I do not harm women.' The glint in his gaze spoke of pride and outrage.

But she'd take no chances. 'In the circumstances I know you'll understand if I reserve the right to protect myself.'

Not by so much as a flicker of his eyelids did he move. Yet his features grew taut, the grooves beside his mouth deepening, the angle of his jaw becoming razor-sharp.

Amir regarded her with stunned curiosity. His word was not enough? He wasn't to be trusted?

Surely she couldn't believe him to be cut from the same cloth as Mustafa and his cronies?

It seemed she could.

She lifted her chin, revealing a slender throat that reminded him of her fragility despite her bone-deep defiance. Luminous skin caught his eye, so at odds with her gaudy make-up.

Something stirred inside. Respect for this woman who didn't realise she had no need to keep fighting.

He thought of the long years he'd spent proving himself again and again, fighting against doubt, scorching disapproval and ever-present prejudice. That determination to keep fighting had got him where he was today. Who was he to insist she give up?

'If it gives you comfort, then by all means keep the knife.'

He paused and smiled, expecting acknowledgment of his gesture. After all, to bear arms in the presence of royalty had been till recently a capital offence.

She remained stony-faced and he was torn between exasperation at her distrust and approval of her determination.

Amir gestured towards the outer wall. 'But don't try attacking one of Mustafa's guards with it. They're trained warriors. They won't hesitate to use maximum force if attacked. You'll come off worst.'

'Tell me something I don't know.' Her eyes sparked fire. 'You call them warriors? Kidnapping an unarmed woman? I thought the men here would have more pride.'

'You're right. Their behaviour blemishes honour.'

The mark branded him too. She'd been in *his* kingdom

when abducted. It sickened him that she'd been plucked from his country and subjected to this.

'Mustafa's men will do what Mustafa tells them to.'

'And you?'

She went too far this time.

'Ms Denison.' His voice rang with hauteur. 'I give my word you have nothing to fear from me. The first I knew of your presence was when you were brought to me at the feasting tent.'

'I...' She faltered and her gaze dipped. 'I see. Thank you.'

Like a balloon pricked by a pin, she seemed to deflate before his eyes. Instantly, regret lashed him. Where was his control? Strive as he might to reassure, his reactions to Cassandra Denison were too raw and unpredictable.

How to gentle her and win her trust?

He had a lifetime's experience in pleasuring women. His lovers were well satisfied. But since adolescence females had pursued him. All he'd had to do was reach out and select the one he wanted. He treated them well, but he'd never had to exert himself to win a woman's trust.

How was he to deal with this woman who defied yet intrigued him? A woman so reluctantly dependent on him?

CHAPTER THREE

'WHY isn't it so simple?'

'Pardon?'

Cassie struggled to sound calm. 'Getting me away from here. You said it's not that simple.'

'That's right.' He poured himself a drink, then raised a golden goblet to his lips.

Frowning, Cassie looked away to the table between them. There was something disturbingly intimate about watching the strong muscles of his burnished throat as he tipped his head back to drink.

Was it the stress of her situation that made her so hyperalert? Or the intimacy of this quiet lamplit haven, so peaceful after her recent trauma?

Slowly he lowered the goblet, and she had the unnerving feeling he was preparing to break bad news.

'I've just arrived and I won't be leaving for a week.'

Cassie nodded. 'And…?'

'And you will have to remain here till then.'

'No way!' On surging outrage she rose, only to subside again when he held out an arm to bar her way. He didn't touch. His hand stopped centimetres from hers. But his expression had its effect. 'If you expect me to wait around here a whole week—'

'That's exactly what I expect, Ms Denison. When my negotiations are over I'll escort you to safety. In the meantime, so long as you remain in this tent, you are under my protection. No one will touch you while you are mine.'

Cassie's eyes rounded. *His.*

A bolt of electricity zapped her.

It wasn't news. That scene in the other tent had been brutally clear, despite the language barrier. Yet to hear him spell it out was too much.

'I'm not yours.' Her voice rose. 'I'm not *any* man's.'

He shook his head. 'As far as Mustafa and everyone else in this camp are concerned you belong to me.'

'That's barbaric!'

What century did he think this was?

He shrugged. 'Of course it is. Mustafa thinks to shore up his position by acts of bravado and posturing.' Dark eyes dropped for a moment to her voluminous cloak, but she suspected it wasn't coarse wool he pictured in his head. A tremor ran through her as she remembered his gaze on her bare skin. 'The man has no subtlety.'

Out of nowhere heat washed her. She only just stopped herself wondering what sort of subtleties the Sheikh of Tarakhar preferred.

'But you can't expect me to stay here!'

'I cannot cut this visit short.'

'Not even to rescue a woman in distress?' Cassie never thought she'd play the helpless female, but her situation was dire.

He spread his hands, drawing her gaze to long, capable fingers and strong wrists.

'I'm here to put an end to the sort of border raid to which you fell victim. If diplomacy fails force will be needed. I'm sure you'll understand my preference not to risk the lives of my citizens unless absolutely necessary.'

At his words she raised her head and found her gaze captured.

'I cannot risk what's happened to you happening to anyone else.'

Cassie sat back on her heels. She applauded his purpose. Yet she had to fight to suppress a demand that he take her away from here now—this instant!

'But even if you're staying here I could—'

'What?' His eyebrows arrowed down and his lips thinned. 'Find your own way to safety?'

Did he have to sound so dismissive? She wasn't that naïve. 'Perhaps some of your people could take me.'

Already he was shaking his head. 'I only have a small staff with me and all are required here.' He paused. 'I regret it, but your only option is to leave when I do.'

Cassie clamped her mouth shut and looked away, lest he see the desperation in her eyes.

'This isn't as I'd wish it either.' His voice dropped. 'But it's the only way. Look at me, Cassandra.'

Startled by the sound of her name on his lips, she swung round. 'Cassie.'

'Cassie, then.' Eyes as black as the midnight desert sky bored into hers. She had the unnerving sensation he looked deep into her soul. 'You will forgive my need for absolute honesty?'

'I'd prefer it.' Knowledge was strength. She needed to know where she stood.

He nodded. 'It's essential the camp believes I am content with this arrangement. And that you accept it.'

Her eyes widened as his meaning sank in.

'Should they believe otherwise, Mustafa will give you to someone else and find me a replacement companion. Or keep you for himself.' Dark eyes pinioned hers. 'Do you want to risk that?'

Dread coursed through her veins and she shuddered, remembering the avid faces of the all-male crowd who'd watched as she was presented like some trophy to this man.

Reluctantly she shook her head. She'd stay. For now.

* * *

Half an hour later Cassie stood rigid, eyes fixed on a wall hanging of a courtyard garden with fountains and ornamental trees and beautiful ladies. One played a stringed instrument, one brushed the long, dark hair of another who lifted a cup daintily to her lips. Yet another picked a blossom with delicate fingers.

'It's a garden of pleasures,' the voice, low and rich, murmured. His breath was a puff of warmth on her bare arm and her skin contracted as if brushed by soft suede.

Cassie cleared her throat. 'Really?' She tried not to notice the way his body heat seemed to inflame her bare skin when he stood so close. Whenever his fingers brushed her bare torso she felt a curious trembling.

'Absolutely. In countries like this a garden is a paradise, a place of bountiful water, of green growing things and beauty.'

Cassie knew he only spoke to keep her mind off the fact that he was having trouble unlocking the long lead to the chain around her waist. Yet she found herself lulled by the tantalising burr of his low voice.

Half an hour of kindness, of reassurance, and her terror had abated. Enough for the rigid tension to seep away and anxiety to drop to a barely there undercurrent.

Now she registered other things. A growing awareness of the man beside her, and of her own body.

Perhaps it was the aftermath of stress that made her so sensitive to his nearness. And to his touch.

'And the women in the picture?' She searched for a way to keep him talking. She told herself it was to keep her mind off the worry that the ancient padlock on the chain would never open. Not because she needed distraction from the feel of his large hands brushing her skin with a delicacy that sent whorls of sensation through her.

'Steady, now. This lock is very stiff. You need to be still.'

Cassie sucked in her breath as he insinuated his fingers beneath the chain at her waist and tried to ease the lock free.

'The women represent the pleasures of the senses. Soothing

music, the scent of blossom, the taste of sweet nectar, the plea-sure of touch and the sight of beauty.'

He tugged, then moved, adjusting his hold, and she hurried into speech. 'That's fascinating. I just thought it was a nice design.'

'It's far more than that. It can be read on several levels.'

She felt the soft brush of his hair on her bare skin as he bent close over the old lock. 'Really? What other meanings does it have?'

One hard shoulder shrugged against Cassie's hip. There was a sound of grating, then at last a click. A moment later he straightened, holding up one end of the long lead chain and its ancient padlock.

He grinned, a three-cornered smile that creased his face in unfamiliar lines and made this autocratic lord of the desert suddenly look younger, more approachable and devastatingly attractive.

Cassie's heart thudded to a quickening pace.

Because the loathsome chain was off. That was all.

'The picture is also a metaphor for the pleasures to be found in a lover.' His eyes held hers and Cassie's breathing shallowed. 'The feel of her soft skin, the sound of her sighs, the feminine scent of her, the pleasure to be found in the sight and the taste of her.'

His gaze dropped to her lips and a tingle of effervescence shot through her blood.

An instant later he'd stepped away, his attention on the chain in his hands. Cassie drew a deep breath, telling herself she was glad he'd moved. Her gaze dropped to the chain and she wrapped her arms around her torso. To be tethered like an animal had been degrading.

'You'll be more comfortable without this.' Anger coloured his voice and his knuckles tightened on the ancient links before he let it fall with a dull thud. 'I will have it removed in the morning.'

Her stomach clenched hard and hope flared at the sense

this man really did take her part. Always she'd fought her battles alone. This time she was grateful for help.

'Thank you, Your Highness.' Was that her voice, so breathless?

His head jerked up and their gazes collided. 'In the circumstances we can drop the formalities. You may call me Amir.'

Cassie swallowed. After all she'd been through why did this simple, sensible offer touch her to the core? Was she so desperate for a friendly face? A gentle tone?

She still felt so…vulnerable.

'Thank you, Amir.' She paused, listening to the sound of his name on her tongue.

'What about this?' She hooked a hand through the finer chain encircling her waist. He followed her gesture, his gaze dropping to her almost bare body. Heat coursed through her. 'Can you get this off?'

He shook his head and slowly lifted his eyes. 'I'd need tools to remove it. Tools I don't have with me.'

Dismay filled her. She'd have to keep wearing it? Unlike the other one, this wasn't heavy but it was a potent reminder of her untenable situation. A slave chain.

Her heady sense of freedom disintegrated as harsh reality returned.

'When we return to Tarakhar it will be a quick matter to remove it.'

Silently Cassie nodded, telling herself she was grateful for what he'd achieved. Suddenly exhaustion crept into her limbs and she felt the last of her energy seep away.

Amir gestured to the massive old-fashioned hip bath the servants had filled with hot water. Curls of steam rose languidly from the surface.

'I'll leave you now to wash.' He turned and was almost out through the door before pausing. 'Call if you need anything.'

By his watch not much time elapsed before she emerged from the bathing room. But it seemed like hours. Hours in which

Amir had soothed his fury by planning suitable punishment for Mustafa and those involved in the kidnapping. Yet Amir's thoughts strayed continually to Cassie Denison's vibrant face, her courage and determination. Her lush body.

Those long minutes working the ancient padlock free of the chain at her waist had been torment. He guessed she'd steeled herself against his touch. He hadn't questioned her yet on how badly she'd been abused by her kidnappers, and bile rose in his throat at the thought of any of Mustafa's rabble laying hands on her.

That was what had made his hands unsteady: anger.

He'd been eager to get the job done, to give her the privacy she needed. Yet he'd been curiously fumble-fingered. It hadn't just been the old lock that had been the problem. His unsteady hands had been as much to blame.

Her innocent questions about the old wall hanging, no doubt scavenged by Mustafa in some raid on an ancient stronghold, had channelled Amir's thoughts in directions that were too intimate for comfort.

He knew the look, scent, sound and feel of her. In one moment of heady madness he'd wondered how she'd taste on his tongue, till he'd pulled himself up short and focused on the lock.

His celibacy these past months told against him, letting his thoughts easily stray to sexual pleasure. It had been too long since he'd taken a woman into his bed.

He breathed deep. His advisors were right. The sooner he married the better.

Mistresses were well and good, but he grew tired of their demands and their grasping eagerness. How long since the pleasure of having beautiful women vie for his attention had begun to pall?

A wife wouldn't cling. A wife would be busy with the royal household, with raising their children. But she'd be there for his comfort too.

He smiled, enjoying the notion.

Till he realised the woman in his imaginings had eyes of deep violet and hair like tumbled corn silk.

The bedroom was still, almost dark but for the dimmed light of a single lamp. Yet Cassie paused on the threshold, her heart thumping.

The bed was massive. Low and wide enough for four. Yet it looked far too full with just one man occupying it.

No matter that he'd given his word. That he'd assured her she was safe. Cassie couldn't share his bed.

A shiver spidered its way down her backbone, drawing her skin taut at the idea. Silently she crept across the carpeted floor to gather up her black cloak. Holding her breath, she reached her other hand to the bed and slid a massive pillow towards her.

He remained oblivious, his chest rising and falling slightly with each breath.

A spurt of indignation filled her that he should be so unaffected by her presence, her story of abduction and ill use, that he'd fallen asleep. Yet it made this easier.

With quick, efficient movements Cassie wrapped the cloak around herself and curled up on a silk carpet beside the bed. She nestled her head on the plump pillow and almost sighed her pleasure. Every bone ached with tiredness.

'You can't sleep there.' The crisp voice came out of the darkness. Instantly she stiffened.

'I prefer to sleep alone.'

'We've been through this, Cassie.' Was that a sigh she heard? 'Still you do not trust me?'

'It's not…' Of course it was. A matter of trust.

But how could she trust this stranger as completely as he expected?

A stranger whose touch had been gentle yet soothingly impersonal as he'd removed that hated lead chain. A stranger whose deep voice and efficient, unfussy care had eased her frayed nerves and given her support when she needed it.

Still—

Her thoughts disintegrated as warmth surrounded her. Strong arms lifted her tight against his solid form.

Terror engulfed her, obliterating her tentative sense of well-being. Cassie fought to escape but could get no purchase on the smooth, hard muscle of his bare torso. Not when his body seemed made of unbreakable steel beneath the warm silk of his skin.

A whoosh of air was expelled from her lungs as he dropped her onto the bed. Cassie barely touched the mattress before she was scrabbling to escape, but he sat beside her, his hip hard against her own, his hold firm as he captured her flailing hands in one of his.

'Enough!' The single word broke through her panicked struggles. 'Enough. You are quite safe.'

Safe? Cassie stared up at a broad, muscled torso dusted with dark hair, to a dangerously angled jaw accentuated by the shadow of stubble. Her heart gave a single lurch. Of fear or something else?

'You can't sleep on the floor. You will sleep here, with me, and you will give the impression, when the servants arrive in the morning, that you are well content. Is that understood?'

Eyes like glittering black jade met hers. 'Cassie? Do you understand? It must appear we spent the night as lovers. For your own safety. Unless you wish to be taken away.'

Cassie swallowed, the movement like scratching sandpaper in her throat. Through the manic pounding of her heart the only sound was her ragged breathing. Fury, she assured herself.

He leaned a fraction closer and the scent of sandalwood tickled her nostrils. 'All right?'

'You give me no choice!' She had no doubt he'd bring her back if she shifted from the bed.

'I'm glad you understand.' Amir moved then, bending away from her and reaching out to something beside the bed.

Cassie froze, wary and at the same time mesmerised by the

shift and bunch of muscles in his torso. She'd never realised how imposing a naked male could be up close.

'Here.' He closed her fingers around something cold. 'My gift to you.' He straightened.

Frowning, Cassie turned from him to look at the heavy object in her hand.

'Hold it like this.' His hand closed around hers and he drew from the scabbard a lethal-looking blade that gleamed wickedly in the lamplight.

'You're kidding!' Cassie's breath sucked in on a hiss of disbelief.

'Keep it with you till I return you to safety. It's far more effective than the paring knife you dropped.'

Stunned, she looked at his smiling mouth, then up to grim eyes that belied his light-hearted tone.

Suddenly she believed. She trusted.

'Sleep with it, Cassie. And if anything frightens you in the night, remember you have this.' On the words he lifted her hand and pressed the tip of the dagger against his chest.

His hand fell away and still the deadly blade rested on his bare, bronzed skin.

Holding the heavy knife took all her strength. Yet within, something surged as she watched him watching her from beneath hooded lids. As she saw the blade glint with every slow rise and fall of Amir's chest.

Her heart squeezed. He gave her not just words, but the power that had been taken from her. The power to protect herself.

The knife wobbled dangerously in her fist and he closed a gentle hand around hers, lowering it to the cool cotton sheet near her shoulder.

'Rest now. No one will harm you.' He released her, his hand hovering a moment as if to stroke her cheek. Then his hand dropped.

His lips thinned and abruptly he stood, towering above her,

his wide square shoulders and tapering waist perfect male symmetry outlined by the single lamp.

Before she could respond he pulled the coverlet over her, and she couldn't help but tense. He stood a moment watching her, then with an abrupt movement bent to tuck in the bedding. A moment later he was striding to his side of the bed.

Cassie's eyes followed him. She took in the power of his lean torso and the powerful buttocks and thighs encased in pale drawstring pants that rode low on his hips. She'd never known a man to look so elemental. So…male.

Heart in mouth, she watched him lift the coverlet on the far side of the bed and slip beneath it. Without a word he turned away from her.

How long she lay there, staring at the golden expanse of his back, Cassie didn't know.

Eventually, despite her determination to remain watchful, her eyelids flickered and her fingers loosened their hold on Amir's knife.

As exhaustion finally claimed her she was aware of a growing sense of peace.

She was almost asleep when her drowsy brain registered why it was she felt so safe. Not because of his words. Nor the concern she'd read in his eyes. Nor the blade he'd given her to defend herself, even against him.

It was the cursory, almost unthinking comfort of that one final action.

How many years had it been since anyone had tucked her into bed for the night? Had showed her such tenderness?

Her heart clutched at the memory, then warmth filled her as she slipped into a dreamless sleep.

She was totally oblivious to the man who turned in the bed and propped himself up to watch her through the night, his brows drawn together in a frown.

CHAPTER FOUR

THE moon rose as Amir rode with Mustafa and his followers through the winding gully back to the encampment.

They'd been out since dawn, occupied by a full day of hawking and riding events designed to entertain and display the prowess of the tough mountain men who gave Mustafa their allegiance. A day designed to exhaust anyone not born to the gritty life of a fighter.

It had been a ploy to give Mustafa the upper hand in the negotiations to come.

He'd miscalculated.

Mustafa knew, of course, about the scandals that had dogged Amir. Who his parents were, his early years of luxury in foreign lands where men weren't men but had grown soft and lazy. Unpromising beginnings for a prince in a land where uncompromising grit and honour were prized.

But his host, like so many before him, hadn't done his homework thoroughly. He'd assumed that old story summed up the Sheikh of Tarakhar.

He hadn't bothered to discover that although Amir's past had shaped him into the man he was today it had made him tougher, stronger, more determined, more focused than any of the so-called warriors surrounding them.

It was Mustafa who sat swaying in his seat, surreptitiously wiping his forehead and growing ill-tempered while Amir rode easily, shoulders straight and mind keen. He could have ridden through the night, still alert and more than capable of dealing with an overblown bully like Mustafa.

He had little respect for the man as anything more than a power broker in an unstable territory. After last night's revelations it had taken all Amir's control not to reveal his fury. The time for that would come. Though Mustafa had received a taste today of the cool hauteur that was a royal sheikh's prerogative.

An image of huge violet eyes flashed into Amir's head.

She'd been asleep when he left. Dead to the world and looking far too pale. In the dawn light, her face free of make-up, she'd looked young and lovely. Even, if that could be believed, innocent.

Till Amir noticed the way her fingers curled around the hilt of her dagger even in sleep.

Emotion surged through him. Something fierce that rippled like a predator on the hunt. Something that craved blood for what had been done to her.

Yet there was also a disturbing sense of frustration. Of helplessness. Feelings he hadn't experienced since boyhood. For, though he wished it otherwise, he couldn't save Cassie Denison yet from the terror that haunted her.

He had obligations to fulfil here. To move precipitately would risk the peace talks and her safety.

Amir's hands tightened on the reins and his horse broke into a canter. Mustafa slowly followed suit, lumbering along like a sack of potatoes instead of the valiant leader of men he styled himself.

Effervescence fizzed in Amir's blood as they rounded a mountain spur and the camp came into view. Soon he'd be able to rid himself, for a while at least, of this unpalatable company.

He assured himself it wasn't eagerness he felt at the prospect of seeing Cassandra.

How many hours had he lain awake watching her? Sifting her words for truth? Letting his gaze trail over skin that he knew was soft as rose petals, hair like rays of sunlight, a delicate jaw that also spoke of obstinacy, and the most passionate mouth he'd ever seen?

Amir stopped his thoughts in an instant, recognising them as weakness.

He did not cultivate weakness. From the age of eleven he'd had to be better, stronger, tougher than his peers. It hadn't been good enough to succeed—he'd had to excel. That had required absolute commitment and focus.

The women in his life, pleasing through they were, fulfilled a very specific role. He couldn't remember ever being kept awake by the need simply to watch one sleep.

He'd opened his mouth to suggest to Mustafa that they commence discussions after dinner when a shout rent the air. There was a flurry of movement. Figures converged in the direction of his guest quarters, set away from the rest of the camp.

Instantly Amir was galloping out of the darkness towards the compound, his sixth sense urging speed.

Streaking ahead of the rest of the party, he thundered down, drawing his horse to an impossible shuddering stop metres from his tent, where cloaked figures surged and writhed.

'Enough!' The command cut the night air, clearing the space before him. Startled faces peered up and were quickly averted as the men of the camp bowed their way backwards.

Yet the tussle before him continued. Two figures, unevenly matched, grappled right up against his tent. The smaller one fought like a demon, aiming vicious kicks and cleverly leveraging the other's vast weight against him in a sudden move that almost felled the bigger man. But the hulking guard saved himself at the last moment. There was a gasp of pain and a hoarse chuckle as the smaller of the figures bowed back as if stretched taut.

'Release her. *Now*!' Amir was off the horse and striding forward as the larger of the pair raised a whip in one beefy arm.

Fury boiled in Amir's veins. He came in hard, bringing the

big guard down with a sharp punch to the jaw and another to the solar plexus.

Quick. Contained. Lethally effective. Though Amir retained enough control to do no more than stop the aggressor in his tracks. It was more difficult than he'd expected to stifle the urge for violent retaliation. The need to avenge Cassie was a roaring tide in his blood.

The man was easily recognisable as the one who'd led Cassie into the feasting tent last night. The gaoler she'd flinched from. The man who'd left his mark on her skin.

Anger scythed through Amir's belly.

He gathered Cassie to him. Despite the enveloping cloak it could be no other. Her size and proximity to his tent made it inevitable. Who else would have the temerity to keep fighting so desperately against the biggest, most brutal guard in Mustafa's retinue?

As he drew her in, close within the curve of his arm, every sense confirmed her identity.

How could a woman he barely knew feel so familiar? It wasn't merely that she fitted perfectly, tucked under his chin, her arms snaking around his waist as if for support. It was something indefinable that stirred unaccustomed sensations.

A need to protect. A desire to comfort.

'Are you all right?'

'Yes.' Her voice was a hoarse gasp that tore at his control. He felt the heat of her heavy breathing through the fine cotton of his clothes and pulled her in tighter.

Nevertheless she stood stiffly, as if poised to repel further attack, every straining muscle tense.

This woman was brave to the point of being foolhardy.

'What possessed you to leave the tent?' She *knew* there were guards. That she'd be stopped if they saw her.

'It was so late I thought you weren't coming back.'

Guilt punched his gut as he thought of the desperation that must have driven her from the tent. *Because of him.* Had she believed he'd gone and left her for Mustafa?

By now the rest of the riders had poured out of the darkness around them.

A low groan sounded from the figure sprawled before them, drawing all eyes as Mustafa dismounted.

'Your guard is overzealous, Mustafa.' Amir projected his voice to carry. It resonated with the weight of his authority. 'He raised his hand to the woman who is mine.'

Cassie peered beneath the hood of her cloak at the throng of riders around them. The smells of sweat, dust and horses filled her nostrils, and in an instant she was back on the deserted road, when raiders had swarmed around the broken-down bus, their eyes hard and their hands rough as they'd yanked her off her feet and away with them.

Fear warred with anger. These were the scum who'd abducted her days ago. Who'd treated her as a possession to be bartered for royal favour!

Despite knowing defeat was inevitable in her tussle with the guard, there'd been a sliver of satisfaction in proving she wasn't quite as defenceless as they'd assumed. One on one it hadn't been the easy victory her captor had thought. She'd seen the surprise and pain in his eyes as he realised his mistake.

But now the defiant surge of adrenalin ebbed and she faced the dangerous consequences of her attempt to escape.

Her arms tightened around Amir. He seemed the one solid point of safety in this dangerous, violent world. His warmth and the muscled solidity of his body anchored her.

Yet she guessed nothing could save her from this mob.

At their head was the man Amir called Mustafa. A tough-built man whose cold eyes had fed her fear last night. He took in the fallen guard, moaning at Amir's feet, then flicked a contemptuous stare in her direction.

Cassie stiffened, refusing to shrink away, though she sensed the rage roaring in him, perilously close to the surface. Retreating from a bully was asking for trouble.

Amir's hand squeezed hers, then he pried her fingers loose and stepped forward. Before she knew what was happening he'd shoved her behind him.

Cassie stared, dumbfounded, at his broad back, his shoulders shielding her from the crowd.

Automatically she moved. She needed to see what was happening, to be ready to put up what fight she could. Her hackles rose at being pushed out of the way.

Yet his hold tightened, forcibly restraining her.

She opened her mouth to object when logic finally reasserted itself. Where were her wits? She had no chance against this crowd. She couldn't fight them all, and she couldn't speak their language to reason or plead.

Cassie's only option was to rely on Amir. He, at least, had their respect.

It was unprecedented to have a champion take charge for her. She wasn't sure how she felt about it. Lost, as if he'd snatched something away from her, yet at the same time touched by the gesture.

There was surprising comfort in Amir's large, warm body shielding her as her heart hammered and her body stiffened from the blows that had rained down.

Staunchly she refused to think of the retribution to come. Because of her, Mustafa's lackey lay writhing in agony.

For a moment she was almost grateful for Amir's broad shoulders blocking the view. His wide-legged stance that spoke of strength and a readiness for action.

The idea of a man putting himself between her and danger seemed impossible. Yet there Amir was: solid and real, drawing all eyes to himself and away from her.

A strange sensation filled her chest—a spreading warmth that countered the chill of dread.

She heard the jingle of a harness and the restless snorts of the horses, but not a whisper from the crowd as Amir and Mustafa talked. Their voices weren't raised. They could have been discussing the weather for all the emotion she heard. But that didn't stop a shiver tripping down her spine.

That look in Mustafa's eyes… Cassie had no doubt he'd make her pay in spades for the damage done to his minion.

She tucked her hand into the sash Amir wore over his robe. To offer silent support or gain comfort?

Still they talked.

Eyes closed, head tilted forward, almost touching Amir's back, Cassie was struck by the beauty of his voice as it flowed, deep and smooth through the night, turning the unfamiliar sounds and rhythms into something arrestingly beautiful.

Finally there was a lull in the discussion and Amir spoke quietly in English. 'Go now. Walk directly to the tent and wait for me inside.'

Her brain numb after standing so long, lost in thought, Cassie opened her eyes and stared at his back. Had he really spoken or was that wishful thinking?

'Cassie!' It was a low hiss of sound. 'Go now. Quietly. Don't run. You're quite safe.'

She swallowed a mirthless laugh at the idea of being safe *here*. Yet without further thought she slid her hand free of his belt and adjusted the cloak more tightly around her. Steeling her nerve, she turned and forced herself to walk slowly towards the tent's entrance.

She'd just got inside when she met the man she'd seen last night at Amir's side, coming the other way. In his hands he carried the long chain Amir had taken off her.

Cassie shrank against the wall of the tent, heart hammering at the sight of it.

The man paused. 'Don't concern yourself, Ms Denison,' he said in fluent English. 'You won't have to worry about this again. His Highness will see to it.' Then he sketched a rapid bow and left before she could find her voice.

Ms Denison.

The title in her own language seemed incongruously formal

after a fight in the dark with a guard and the threatening crowd outside.

It reminded her of the safety she'd left behind in Australia. The foreignness of this wild place.

And her total dependence on the Sheikh of Tarakhar.

Cassie grabbed a tent pole for support as she absorbed the stunning reality of what had just happened.

Amir had done what no man ever had. He'd stood on Cassie's side. He'd done more, literally fighting her battle for her.

The memory of him putting her behind him and facing down that threatening mob made something twist inside.

The men she'd known hadn't been models of virtue. They'd been self-absorbed and anything but honourable. As a result she'd learned self-reliance and distrust young. Cassie never let any man close enough to find out if he had an honourable streak. She no longer believed such a man existed.

It worried her to discover how much she wanted to believe Amir was such a man. He'd come back for her, protected her, putting himself in danger in the process. He'd won her gratitude and respect.

But the hard lessons of youth couldn't be ignored. Would he expect recompense for his protection? Her mouth twisted at the thought, and she knew a twinge of unfamiliar regret that suspicion was so ingrained.

'Cassie?' Amir's deep voice skimmed like hot velvet over her body. 'What's wrong? Are you hurt?' An instant later strong arms enfolded her, sweeping her up against his tall frame.

Her eyes rounded in surprise. She opened her lips to demand he put her down. But she closed them as an unfamiliar sense of wellbeing filled her.

'I'm perfectly fine. I was just thinking.' She told herself she wanted to stand on her own feet despite feeling battered and bruised. Yet his embrace was insidiously comforting. Something she could get too accustomed to.

She needn't have worried. He sat her on the edge of the wide bed and stepped back, well out of arm's length.

Out of sensibility for her situation? The possibility was intriguingly novel. The bud of warmth inside her swelled.

'Thank you,' she murmured, forcing herself to sit straight despite new aches.

'Are you hurt?'

'No.' She lifted her head, meeting a dark gaze that seemed to bore right through her attempt to gloss over her injuries. 'I'm OK.'

Amir's brows arched eloquently, as if he knew just how much pain she'd borne, but he said nothing.

'How about you? Are you injured?' She hadn't seen exactly how he'd taken down the guard.

His mouth turned up at one corner in a lazy smile that tugged something in her chest tight. 'Never better.'

'Good.' She clasped her hands, unsure of the expression in those dark eyes. As an actress she prided herself on her knowledge of body language, but this man was so hard to read!

'Thank you for coming to my rescue.' The words emerged primly, as if she thanked him for a trifling favour, when they both knew that without his intervention she'd have been—

'I told you I'd look after you. Why didn't you believe me?'

Cassie spread her hands. No point saying she'd learnt never to take anyone's promises at face value.

When she'd woken, rested and unharmed in that massive, empty bed, she'd almost wondered if she'd dreamed Amir's presence. But his dagger in her fist had been real. His belongings further proof he'd been there.

'I couldn't be sure. Besides, I've been alone so long I'm used to looking out for myself.'

'You've had a traumatic experience.'

Cassie nodded. She hadn't been talking about just that, but there was no point revealing her isolation had taken a lifetime to grow.

'When I didn't see anyone all day I—'

'No one?' Amir scowled. 'What about servants bringing food and water?'

Cassie shook her head and watched as the lines bracketing his mouth grew deep and fire lit his eyes.

'Go on.' His voice was grim.

'There's nothing more to say. At first it was OK. I felt safe and…comfortable.' Even though she'd chafed at the inaction, waiting for his return when all she wanted was to get away.

'Then, as evening drew in, I started to worry.' She looked away from his sharp scrutiny. No need to tell him she'd thought he'd decided to leave her to her fate. 'I wondered if something had happened to you.'

'And about what would happen to you if it had?'

Quickly she nodded, not wanting to think about it, remembering the savage blows that had rained down on her. She drew a deep breath and shifted to ease the aches in her back and side. 'Finally I gave up waiting. I took your knife and tried to slip out the back of the tent.'

If only she'd done as he'd said—trusted in his word to protect her and stayed where she was. She'd tried. She really had. But as the hours had ticked by it had become increasingly difficult to believe he would return. To believe she could trust him.

'I don't like to think what would have happened if you hadn't rescued me.'

'You are my responsibility.' His tone was matter-of-fact, but there was no mistaking its grim edge. Amir wasn't happy about this situation either.

'I'm…' Cassie shut her mouth before she could blurt out that she was no one's responsibility. She looked after herself! But in her current situation independence was an illusion, possible only with the concurrence of this man. The knowledge ate at her like acid.

Stoically she repressed a shiver.

'You're cold.' He took a step forward, then halted. Cassie

was glad of his distance. This man could crowd her with just a look.

'Your dagger!' She started, suddenly remembering the knife she'd dropped as she'd wriggled from under the tent.

'We'll look for it later.'

'No!' She couldn't have that on her conscience.

In the darkened room last night she'd noticed nothing but the fact he'd trusted her with a blade against his bare skin. That he'd given her the means to protect herself. But today she'd examined the knife and been stunned to discover what looked like an antique heirloom.

The scabbard was encrusted with rubies cut in old-fashioned cabochon style. The blade, wickedly sharp, bore a flourish of exquisite calligraphy near the hilt. The handle was a work of art: an emerald the size of an egg embedded in precious metal.

The thing was probably a national treasure!

Cassie shot to her feet, then paused, a hand going to her lower back as pain slammed through her. That guard had pulled no punches.

'Cassie?'

She forced a taut smile as she turned towards the edge of the tent. 'I'm just a bit stiff.'

'Are you always this stubborn?'

'Always.' What he called stubborn she called getting on with life.

She sensed him just behind her as she searched for the place where she'd wriggled out of the tent. The heat of his big frame so close to her should have disturbed and intimidated after the events of the past few days. Yet strangely she found his nearness comforting. As if nothing could harm her while he was there.

Nonsense! It was absurd wishful thinking. Dangerous thinking.

Yet as she crouched down and investigated the layers of

carpet at the place she'd escaped Cassie found herself grateful for his reassuring presence.

'There.' A long arm reached round her and grabbed the gleaming hilt, half hidden beneath an edge of carpet.

Cassie froze, her pulse rocketing. The sense of being surrounded was suddenly too real and not at all reassuring.

But instead of pressing home his physical advantage Amir stood, then extended his hand to her. 'Here.'

It was on the tip of Cassie's tongue to refuse his help. But grappling with the guard had taken its toll. She felt as if she'd had a run-in with a herd of wild horses.

'Thank you.' Her voice was husky as his hand engulfed hers and he pulled her up. Strange how the touch of that callused hand seemed so much more real than the smooth handshakes of the men she met and worked with in Melbourne.

His was the touch of a hard-working man. A man of decision. Of strength.

Cassie blinked and withdrew her fingers, disturbed at the trend of her thoughts.

'I wouldn't have forgiven myself if anything had happened to it.' She forced herself to turn and meet his enigmatic gaze. 'It must be worth a fortune.'

'Far more than a fortune. Its value is in the fact it's been passed through my family for centuries.'

'Yet you gave it to me?' Cassie frowned, snapping her gaze from his arresting features to the weapon in his hand.

'Your need was greater than mine.'

He made it sound so simple. Yet to trust a stranger, even for a short while, with such an heirloom seemed crazy.

'Here.' He extended his hand, palm open. Light reflected off the gem in the hilt and dazzled her. 'Keep it till you're free.'

For an instant Cassie knew an insane urge to push his hand away and say she felt utterly safe here, with him.

Until she remembered the guards surrounding the tent. The

malice in Mustafa's eyes. She reached for the weapon, her fingers closing around its solidity.

She concentrated on its weight, the protection it represented, and tried to ignore the ripple of sensation that coursed through her when her hand touched Amir's.

CHAPTER FIVE

AMIR was reading a report on a new gas pipeline when he sensed her enter. Her bare feet made no sound on the carpet, and without the jingling coin belt there was no obvious sign of her presence.

Yet he sensed her. *Felt* her here, in his domain.

Deliberately Amir forced himself to read another long paragraph. The pipeline was far more important to him, to his plans for Tarakhar, than the woman who'd finally emerged from the bathroom.

Yet the words ran together, jumbling into incoherence as he pretended not to notice her. Finally he thrust aside the papers and looked up. His breath seared his lungs.

She stood defiantly, as if daring him to comment. Her chin was up, her eyes narrowed, and her feet planted a little apart.

In other circumstances Amir would have warned her that the spark of challenge in her eyes, far from dousing male interest, only heightened the delicious temptation of the picture she made.

Gone was the dancing girl outfit. Instead she wore a collarless white shirt of his.

Whatever misguided sympathy had possessed him to offer his clothes for her to wear after her bath?

But how could he have known that Cassie wearing his shirt would be one of the sexiest sights he'd ever encountered?

Heat coiled low as his eyes flicked over her.

The cotton covered her almost to the knees. She'd rolled

the sleeves up and the material hung loose around her. Yet the slit neck dived to her cleavage. The hint of a shadow there intrigued him as she moved restlessly.

Worse, the cotton clung to her breasts, firm and high even without the bustier. As he watched, her nipples peaked, thrusting against the fine material.

Amir swallowed, his mouth drier than the great interior desert, as he dragged his gaze down to shapely legs and dainty feet.

Less is more.

It was true. The dancing costume had been blatantly sexy, designed to appeal to the basest of male hungers.

Yet the simplicity of what she wore now was more erotic than anything he could recall. Or was that because he knew beneath his shirt she was naked?

Quickly Amir looked away.

'I have something for you.' His voice was husky and he reached for water, telling himself he was dry after a day in the saddle.

'A pair of shoes?'

His lips curved at her undaunted humour. 'I'm afraid even I can't conjure a pair small enough to fit you.'

He shoved aside the realisation that he liked her barefoot in his rooms. No doubt the sight appealed to some deeply buried primitive instinct for dominance.

'Though I could arrange a smaller shirt if you like.' Faruq was much smaller than he. Surely one of his shirts—?

'No. Thank you. This is fine.'

Amir nodded and put the goblet down. Even as he'd suggested it part of him had protested at the idea of her wearing another man's clothes.

What sort of crazy possessiveness was that?

Cassie Denison evoked primal responses no civilised man should feel.

Amir frowned. He'd had lovers since his teens. Beautiful,

accommodating women who gave him everything he desired. He couldn't recall feeling possessive about a woman before.

'What is it? The thing you have for me?' She sounded tentative and Amir smiled.

'Liniment.' He let himself turn back to her, careful to keep his gaze on her face. Bare of make-up, her cheeks pink from a steamy bath and her hair pulled back in a long, gleaming plait of gold, she looked impossibly alluring.

His mouth tightened.

'Liniment?' Her head tilted to one side.

He nodded. 'You're bruised. This will help. One of my aides provided it.' Ever prepared, Faruq had brought it for his own use, knowing that this time diplomacy entailed days of hard riding to which he, unlike Amir, wasn't accustomed.

'I just rub it in?'

Amir nodded slowly, the glitch in his plans only now dawning on him. 'You may need help.'

'I'm sure I'll manage,' she said hurriedly, reaching out a hand.

His fingers closed around the small pot. 'Where are you hurt?' He watched her eyes dip. 'Cassie?'

She shrugged. 'My hip. I told you, I can manage.'

'And your back.' He remembered the way pain had streaked across her features when she'd suddenly risen and how her hand had shot to her lower back.

He dragged in a deep breath, reviewing the few staff members he'd brought with him and discounting each in turn. To confront her with a man she'd never met was asking too much. There must be women in the camp somewhere, but he didn't trust any of Mustafa's people to care for Cassie.

Lead settled in his gut as he realised he had no choice. So much for his altruistic gesture!

'Get into bed, on your stomach. I'll see to it.'

'I told you I'll be fine. I—'

'Don't try my patience, Cassie.' He didn't raise his voice. He didn't need to. He'd perfected the voice of authority long ago. 'You'll feel worse without treatment and this will allow you to sleep.'

He met her wide eyes and a jolt of pure energy arced through him. 'It's just liniment, Cassie. Nothing else.'

She drew a slow breath, then another, and Amir kept his eyes trained on her face. Finally her gaze slid away. As if she was the one whose thoughts betrayed a baser self!

Without a word she slipped into the bed.

Out of the corner of his eye he saw a flurry of pale legs, and heat exploded through him, slicing through his good intentions.

He waited a full minute before getting to his feet, gathering himself. His lips twisted in a travesty of a smile. When had touching a beautiful woman become an ordeal?

Since he'd become responsible for her.

He knew the old traditions. The belief that if you saved a life that person belonged to you. For a second he lingered over the notion of Cassie as *his*, available to gratify his every pleasure. Yet it wasn't so simple. His responsibility for her weighed on his conscience.

Slowly he paced to the bed. She lay with her head turned away, the covers just reaching the dip at the small of her back.

'Lift the shirt higher.' His voice was gravel, and swallowing was painful as he watched her wriggle under the covers and then tug the cotton high enough to reveal a narrow strip of pale skin.

'Good.' Amir kept his tone brisk as he sat on the edge of the bed and took the lid off the pot.

He turned his mind to massages he'd received, the placement of hands, the pressure on tight muscles, hoping to dredge up enough knowledge to do this right.

The only trouble was, in his experience, such hands-on treatment usually led to other, utterly sensual pleasures.

Cassie caught her lip between her teeth as she waited, every sense achingly aware, for him to touch her.

Was she a fool, trusting him like this?

Yes, he'd been her protector, her saviour. Even now her heart tumbled over itself as she remembered the way he'd faced that mob, putting himself between them and her.

But to place herself in a position of weakness before any man was anathema to her.

She remembered Curtis Bevan's hand thrusting into her school shirt, only minutes after he'd left her mother, and bile rose. She recalled the last slimy proposition she'd received from a director eager for her to have a 'private audition'. The salacious expressions on Mustafa's men just yesterday as she'd stood before them, more than half naked.

No matter how much those new injuries ached, she was a fool! No way could she put her faith in any man to—

Her instinctive movement stilled as something warm and wet was slapped onto her bare skin.

'I've changed my mind. I don't—'

'Just relax.' His voice was a low rumble from above, but it was his hand at her waist that stopped her moving. Large, gentle, almost tentative, it shaped the curve of her lower back, smoothing ointment from side to side.

Each muscle tensed. She was too aware of his hip against her thigh, separated only by the bedcover, the fact that beneath the cotton of his shirt she was naked.

'Stop tensing your muscles or this will hurt.'

'I don't know how.'

Was that a sigh she heard? 'Never mind. Just try to clear your head. Think of something pleasant.'

Pleasant? Desperately she tried to relax and conjure the memory of her last encore at a live performance.

Two hands caressed her back now, moving in tandem, thumbs pressing and palms pushing in a rhythmic movement that suddenly had her thinking instead of chocolate. Lush, soft truffles that melted on your tongue. Liquid dark chocolate that swished lusciously when stirred.

His touch gentled at the place where the pain was worst,

then smoothed in again where she'd felt the strain of muscle spasm on one side.

Cassie's eyes flickered shut as the steady swirl of his fingers deepened and a puff of breath escaped her.

'Oh.'

Instantly he stilled. 'I hurt you?'

'No.' Cassie stretched, her body weighted yet limber from his ministrations. 'It's…good.'

Liar. It was fantastic. So fantastic that when she felt his hands on her again Cassie was hard put to ignore the delicious swirling sensation in her belly, the trembling effervescence in her blood, the way she wanted to arch into his touch and purr her delight.

'Which hip?' He sounded different. Curiously strained.

'Right.'

A moment later he slid the sheet down a fraction on one side, but not enough to reveal her buttocks.

A hiss of air made her stiffen.

'What is it?'

'You'll be sore for a while. That's a nasty bruise.' This time there was no massage, just a whisper-soft caress as he stroked ointment over her injury.

'Where else?'

For a moment Cassie debated, then gave in. It was clear Amir had no ulterior motives. To him this was a chore. Not by a centimetre had his touch strayed.

'If you wouldn't mind…a little higher up my back?'

Wordlessly he lifted the shirt over her shoulderblades. Instinctively Cassie pressed her breasts further down into the bed.

Then his hands were on her, working magic into muscles tense with days of strain. There was a little pain as he worked the stiffness free, but above all there was lovely, drugging pleasure. She could lie here all night if only he'd keep doing this.

'You're very good with your hands.'

'Thank you.' He sounded terse. Obviously he'd had enough of playing the masseur.

'You can stop now.' Yet even as she said it Cassie found herself arching her spine and pressing her forehead into the pillow in response to the lush waves of pleasure radiating from his capable hands.

'In a minute.' Slowly he worked his way down, past the chain encircling her waist to her lower back.

A strange hollow ache began deep in her abdomen, an edginess that made her shift her hips and legs restlessly. She sought for distraction.

'Why did that man take the chain from the tent tonight?'

'Faruq?' Once more Amir's hand barely skimmed her sore hip, gently smoothing in ointment before returning to massage her back. 'He's here with me. He came to fetch the chain for the guard who attacked you.'

'Why? What's happened to him?'

'Nothing yet. Though it seems he's still in a lot of pain.'

No mistaking the satisfaction in Amir's voice. She was human enough to feel it too, knowing the man who'd tormented and hurt her suffered for what he'd done.

'And later?'

'He'll come with us. Mustafa has handed him to me for punishment.'

'Mustafa wouldn't have liked that.' Cassie recalled the raw fury on his face as he'd seen his henchman writhing at her feet.

'What Mustafa likes is of no consequence. The man attacked my woman. He must pay.'

Strangely this time Cassie didn't feel the same blistering anger at being labelled Amir's woman. Probably because she was melting in a puddle of sheer pleasure.

'What will happen to him?' She shivered, thinking of the barbarous world she'd entered. 'Will he be beaten?'

'Nothing so simple or quick.' Amir's voice was like honed steel. 'There's a huge construction project on the outskirts of my capital. It's all high-tech building processes, but there's scope for old-fashioned hard labour under strict supervision. Your friend will be up before dawn every day, digging, carrying, cutting stone. He'll stop only after the sun goes down. He will learn the hard way that violence against women is not to be tolerated.'

Cassie swung her head round to look into the dark face above her.

Amir's eyes glowed with a heat she hadn't seen before. Anger at the guard, she told herself.

Yet something in his scrutiny made her gaze slide away, warmth rising in her cheeks. She stared at the throb of Amir's pulse strong and fast at the base of his throat. She watched, fascinated, as the grimness left his mouth, his lips relaxing into sculpted sexiness.

Her breath snagged as the idea hit that his focus wasn't on the guard. It was on her.

A trembling started deep inside.

She licked dry lips. 'You're going to a lot of trouble with him.'

Amir shrugged. 'He harmed you. Deliberately. He did far more than just stop you escaping.' Amir's fingers splayed at her waist, insinuating themselves under the chain, a tangible reminder that as far as the rest of the camp was concerned she was here to please Amir.

Startled, she looked up again.

A flash of something lit his eyes. A flash that reverberated through her, drawing her nipples into tight buds and shooting a wire of tension through her abdomen, right down to the juncture of her thighs.

'What will he be building?' Her voice sounded thready, as if coming from a long distance away.

'A hospital for women and children.' Amir's mouth tilted up into a smile that suddenly dispersed the tension clogging the air between them. 'Fitting, don't you think?'

* * *

She shouldn't feel so relaxed and content. Her overwrought brain tried to remind her danger was all around, not least in the man prowling across the room to the far side of the vast bed.

But it was no good. Amir's touch, his massage, his words of reassurance and above all his presence, made her feel…safe.

Her gaze followed him. She assured herself it was natural to be curious. As for the way she followed each sleek line of that bare, powerful torso, the play of light over shifting muscles, the contrast between broad, straight shoulders and the bunch of tight buttocks beneath those loose trousers… Cassie swallowed. There was nothing wrong with acknowledging a rare example of prime masculinity, was there?

Yet a niggle of disquiet stirred.

She'd never been one to ogle a good-looking man. Not just because in her experience most of them were utterly self-absorbed.

What was it about Amir that awakened dormant feminine responses? That made her pulse quicken watching his loose-limbed stride, seeing the smattering of black hair across his broad chest as he turned?

Dark eyes snared hers across the width of the bed and her heart stuttered.

'Do you want the lamp left on again tonight? Would you feel safer?'

The jitter of response in her belly eased at his prosaic words.

She'd been mistaken. There was nothing in his look but concern. Cassie strove to smother a twinge of illicit disappointment.

She didn't *want* his interest! She was *grateful* he saw her merely as a responsibility!

'I'm OK. You can turn the light off.' She hadn't even realised he'd slept last night with the light burning. Again, his consideration for her struck home.

'If you're sure.' He turned away and a moment later the room was plunged into blackness.

Cassie blinked, as if that would let her see, but there was nothing—only the sound of Amir putting something on the small table beside the bed. She heard the whisper of the covers being drawn back, then the rustle of sheets as he slipped into bed.

Her heart hammered as reality hit her anew. She was sharing a bed with a stranger. A virile, powerful man. Surreptitiously her fingers slid under the pillow till they touched hardness, the golden hilt of that magnificent dagger.

Strangely that didn't ease Cassie's agitation. She couldn't imagine needing a weapon to protect her from Amir. What concerned her was her unwanted awareness of him. The fact that she was torn between a desire to curl up on the far side of the tent, as far away as possible, and to snuggle into him, letting his strong arms encircle her and keep her safe.

'Are you sure this is necessary?' She kept her tone prosaic. 'There were no servants here today. No one will know if we don't spend the night together in the same bed.' Cassie drew a shallow breath. 'I could sleep over—'

'No.' The single word silenced her. 'From now on you will be served as an honoured guest. I've made that clear to Mustafa. Besides...' He paused. 'You might as well be comfortable. After your ordeal you need rest.'

Silence engulfed them. Cassie focused on slowing her breathing, trying to relax. But meditation was impossible when even in the darkness she could picture with perfect mouth-watering clarity the honed power of Amir's form.

'Cassandra?' His voice came out of the darkness, low and soft, a burr that brought every sense alert.

'Yes?' She frowned, wondering at Amir's use of her full name.

'I *will* punish that man for beating you.' Amir paused long enough for Cassie to wonder if he sought the right words. 'If there is anything else he needs to be brought to account for you must tell me.'

Cassie frowned. How was she to know what other crimes the guard had committed? She'd be surprised if he hadn't assaulted others. The man was a bully.

'Cassie?'

'I don't know...'

'Or the others who brought you here. If they have harmed you in any other way they will be made to pay.' The lethal softness of his tone finally penetrated. It was a voice that, for all its control, spoke of barely contained fury.

Cassie was grateful for the enveloping darkness that hid her fiery cheeks as his meaning became clear. 'They didn't touch me like that.'

'You mustn't be ashamed.' His voice curled around her, warm and considerate. 'If they forced—'

'No!' she gasped. 'No, they didn't.' She paused, but the urge to talk outweighed her embarrassment. Here in the inky stillness it was easier to spill her fears. Easy to take comfort in Amir's presence, just out of reach.

'I was sure they'd rape me.' Her breath stalled on remembered terror. 'I expected it every hour. Whenever the guard came to the tent. When he looked at me like that...'

Cassie's words petered out as her mind filled with an image of the man's knowing smirk, the way just a look could make her feel unclean.

'And when they took me to the big tent last night I thought...'

'Of course you did.'

Cassie heard what sounded like swearing under his breath, heartfelt and violent. Yet this time it didn't make her cringe. His anger on her behalf was balm to her lacerated soul.

'You were brave last night, Cassandra. A lot of women would have been too terrified to defend themselves, much less attack.'

'Cassie,' she said. When he called her by her full name an unsettling frisson channelled through her.

'Cassie.'

She loved the way he said her name. It seemed to vibrate across her skin in his impossibly deep, soft tones.

'I'm sorry I hurt you.' She'd never properly apologised. She'd been so busy focusing on herself that she'd let him tend to her injuries when all the time his had been potentially lethal. 'If the knife had gone in further…' She shuddered at the enormity of what she'd almost done.

'It didn't. It wouldn't have.' He sounded so matter-of-fact.

Her lips twisted. 'It came close.'

'Yes. You're a woman to be reckoned with.'

Cassie's heart skipped. Of all the things he could have said *that* was the nicest compliment of all to a woman who'd spent her early years being dismissed or excluded. Who'd had to fight for everything she had and was.

'Does it hurt?'

'I'd forgotten about it.'

Sure. He'd been too busy tending to her hurts and felling bullies with just a punch to be concerned about a dagger cut to his throat.

'Remind me never to anger you when we're sharing fruit.'

A gurgle of laughter bubbled in Cassie's throat, easing her tension. It was the first time she'd felt light-hearted in days. It seemed a lifetime and it felt so good.

'Thank you, Amir.'

Silence. 'There's no need for thanks, Cassie.'

She slid her hand out from under the pillow and flexed her fingers where they'd stiffened around his knife. 'There's every need.'

CHAPTER SIX

CASSIE savoured the crisp mountain air and the spicy scent of fresh vegetation. After being cooped up in a tent, however luxurious, the freedom of being outdoors was magic. Even though the freedom was illusory.

She glanced at the rocks to her left. Somewhere hidden from sight were the guards, there to protect their royal guest and, no doubt, to ensure *she* didn't escape.

'You like the view?' Amir's voice came from beside her, and inevitably heat spooled through her veins. That low, sexy rumble undermined every barrier she tried to maintain.

She turned, noticing how, as usual, Amir kept his distance. More than necessary for propriety. Clearly he sent a message. That despite their forced proximity he had no interest in her person.

Had he recognised the dangerous laxness that had invaded her body at his massage? The heady longing for more?

'It's magnificent,' she said quickly, cutting off that line of thought. 'Thank you for bringing me here.'

He spread his hands. 'Your confinement must be difficult to bear.' His eyes met hers and she felt that familiar jolt. 'I only wish I could do more.'

The grim lines around his mouth accentuated what she already knew. Amir was a man of action, used to resolving problems and no doubt getting his own way. It must gall him that he couldn't get her away from the camp immediately.

'I understand. Time looking after me is time away from

your negotiations. The more delays, the longer before we leave.'

A slight lift of dark eyebrows signified his surprise.

Had he thought she didn't understand the situation? She'd little to do but think about it through the long, lonely hours.

'I appreciate the trouble you've taken to arrange this.' Not only Mustafa's guards but Amir's men were on duty for this short excursion. 'But, believe me, the sooner you finish your work here the happier I'll be.' Despite Amir's protection Cassie wouldn't be truly safe till she was in Tarakhar.

She let her gaze drift to the magnificent vista, like a 3D map before her. 'So where's the border?'

Amir pointed to the foot of the escarpment. 'Beneath this range. All that—' his sweeping hand encompassed a vast plain of patchwork fields '—is Tarakhar.'

'It looks prosperous.' She recalled the route her bus had taken. 'I'd expected it to be arid.'

'Further south is the Great Interior Desert. One of the harshest environments in the world, yet still nomads exist on its fringes.'

Amir described his country, from its fertile valleys to its deserts and rugged mountains, with an enthusiasm that made her almost jealous. She enjoyed Melbourne, its bustle and vibrant arts culture, but she'd never experienced this love of place so clearly evident in Amir.

Gilded by the sun, what she could see of Tarakhar looked idyllic.

'What's that, crisscrossing the plain? They're not roads, are they?' Cassie caught the glint of water.

'Irrigation channels. That's the secret to the region's prosperity. Water from the mountains is fed through channels, some of them underground, in a system that's hundreds of years old.'

Amir led her to the comfortable folding chairs his staff had set out. Nearby a table groaned with food.

* * *

Faruq had excelled himself, Amir noted, eyeing delicacies to tempt the most jaded appetite.

Not that Cassie's appetite was jaded. She wasn't greedy, but her enjoyment of local dishes pleased him. Or maybe it was that he liked watching her eat. The way she savoured each taste. Her neat economy of movement.

She looked up to find him watching. A hint of colour tinted her cheeks and she turned away. Proof that she had no interest in him sexually. It was a timely reminder.

'I hadn't expected it to be so beautiful,' she said, looking at the distant view.

'You really do like it then?' Strange how her simple praise delighted him. He'd imagined her experiences would prejudice her. That she wouldn't see the beauty he did. But Cassie wasn't the sort to let bitterness take hold. She resented the wrongs done to her, but at core she seemed positive, vibrant and surprisingly strong.

'I enjoyed the little I saw from the bus too. And the people are very friendly.'

'Hospitality comes naturally to the Tarakhans.'

Cassie looked at the massive feast spread between them and laughed, a short peal that seemed to scintillate in the dusky air. It drew a reluctant smile from him and threatened to shatter the formality between them.

Amir walked a fine line. He needed to put her at ease and remedy as far as possible the trauma of her abduction. Yet getting close was dangerous. Already they were too intimate for comfort. Safer by far if he kept their dealings on a casual yet slightly distant footing.

Grudgingly he stifled the urge to hear that laugh again. To discover more about his fascinating companion.

So…nothing else personal.

'Let me tell you about those canals…'

* * *

Amir lay on his side, watching another dawn filter through the tent walls.

Another night without sleep, his mind in turmoil.

He shifted slightly and winced at the brush of cotton against his heated skin. Silently he cursed the need to wear loose trousers. But preserving Cassie's modesty and her sense of security was paramount.

Besides, it wasn't the restriction of fine cotton against aroused flesh that tortured him. It was Cassie.

Bad enough when she lay in the dark on the far side of the bed, her chuckle like the ripple of cool oasis water against hot skin, her breathless husky voice like the whisper of a zephyr through palm trees on a sultry night.

Each word, every action, reinforced the courage in her, commanding his respect.

Yet he had no difficulty picturing her smooth pale limbs, her forbidden curves and hollows. His fingers flexed at the memory of her skin under his hands as he massaged her. So supple, inviting and responsive. Had she realised she'd curled into his touch like a cat arching into a caress?

But he'd withstood temptation. It was this torture that had him at the edge of his tether.

In her sleep Cassie had abandoned her side of the bed and sought his warmth. She lay spooned behind him, her breasts cushioning his back, the heat at the juncture of her thighs warming his buttocks, her legs aligned with his. Her fingers splayed possessively over the taut muscle of his abdomen.

He fought the impulse to flex his hips, tilt his groin so her hand slipped and he felt her fingers *there*, where he wanted her most.

How had curiosity turned to fascination, fascination to desire in a few short days?

Amir drew a shuddering breath and tried to focus on something else. But Cassie chose that moment to sigh and wriggle closer, her warm breath hazing his back, her lips moving in innocent caress against his skin.

There was nothing innocent about her mouth. Even bereft of make-up she had the most sinfully sexy lips. Full, pouting, slightly downturned at the edges, giving her mouth a sulky look that stirred all sorts of libidinous thoughts.

Amir shuddered as desire racked him.

How many more nights of this would he have to endure?

It did no good to rationalise his reaction by remembering he hadn't taken a lover in months. He wanted to roll her over, tug her beneath him and give free rein to the hunger that ravaged him.

But he wouldn't. He couldn't. She'd been traumatised and was under his protection. She trusted him. *That* was what gave him strength to withstand temptation.

Strange that even the thought of his approaching nuptials did nothing to douse his need.

CHAPTER SEVEN

AMIR slammed to a stop in the doorway between the entrance and the main chamber of the tent.

He hadn't allowed himself time today to dwell on Cassie, keeping himself busy with the intricate give and take of negotiations with a wily opponent and the slow pace of formal hospitality.

Yet he hadn't been able to rid himself of that sizzle of awareness. The knowledge that when he returned to his quarters *she'd* be there.

For days he'd behaved impeccably, honourably, despite the arousal twisting him in knots. Despite the lack of sleep that, instead of fatiguing him, focused his brain more sharply on Cassie.

And now—this!

His eyes widened as he saw her in the centre of the room. She wore again that skimpy dancer's outfit as she stretched and twisted in a show of supple strength that made his unruly brain imagine another form of exercise altogether.

He tried to clear his throat, watching as she straightened, turned, then dropped to the ground, her legs opening in perfect splits before she leant to one side, hands around her foot, forehead to her knee.

Desire surged. He wanted her wrapped around him, those pale legs locking tight and her head thrown back in abandon.

He wanted—

'Amir!' A smile lit her face, pleasure making her remarkable eyes glitter before she ducked her gaze to focus on his collarbone.

That still intrigued him—the way a woman so feisty and strong, who'd faced him down like a haughty empress when she'd been brought to him in chains, had for days avoided his gaze.

As if despite her physical courage and her impressive independence there lurked a woman unsure of herself with a man.

Or a woman aware of his unspoken tension.

He paced into the room, letting the curtain drop behind him.

Cassie scrambled to her feet, acutely aware these clothes revealed too much flesh.

Conscious too that something was wrong. Amir's jaw was sharply defined, his shoulders rigid, as if every muscle drew tight. The way his eyes glittered, bright with a fierce light she couldn't name, sent her pulse racing.

'What's happened?'

He shrugged and moved further into the room. 'Nothing. More talk. Offer and counter-offer. Courtesy and ritual.' He flexed his shoulders and a fleeting smile lit his face. 'It's a tedious business. But necessary.'

Cassie frowned. She was conscious of the burdens Amir carried. But he shouldered them with an ease that made her forget sometimes he was ruler of a wealthy kingdom, responsible for the wellbeing of millions.

With her here he couldn't even enjoy privacy after a long day.

She reached for her voluminous cloak, for the first time truly registering the inconvenience she was to him and wishing she could spirit herself away. Grateful as she was for his protection, she'd been too wrapped up in her own fears to consider how little he must want her here.

She spent her time fighting boredom and the inevitable anxiety, knowing the tent was surrounded by armed guards— some of them men who'd abducted her. She spent too much time thinking about Amir. But her thoughts hadn't been about the inconvenience she caused him.

'Are you a dancer?' His question jerked her head up.

For days they'd kept their conversation impersonal, centred on the needs of the moment. As if by mutual agreement their difficult situation would be made easier if they kept their distance. Cassie was sure that was why he spent so little time in his quarters.

Yet despite that Amir was the focus of her waking thoughts as well as her dreams. Her heart quickened in his presence and a hot, unsettled feeling flickered low inside if she inadvertently caught his eye.

'No, I'm not a dancer.' Apart from a lack of talent she wasn't built for it. Cassie had too many curves. But she wasn't about to draw Amir's attention to her overripe dimensions. Bad enough that he'd had an eyeful just now.

The thick cloak settled around her shoulders, scratchy but concealing.

'They looked like dance exercises.' He stopped in front of her and Cassie looked up into his bold, gorgeous face.

A white-hot sizzle of awareness sheared through her. It grew stronger, this discomforting reaction, every time he looked at her. She just hoped he had no inkling of what she felt whenever he drew close.

'I did a little dance years ago, but there's pilates and yoga thrown in. I need something to keep me occupied. I'm climbing the walls with nothing to do.'

Amir had brought no books or papers in English that she could use to occupy herself. Alone each day, the time dragged. She'd written long letters on paper Amir had provided to send to friends when she got away from here. But she'd finished those. Today she'd found herself counting the tassels on the silk wall hangings.

She was going stir crazy. Was it any wonder her thoughts circled back to him?

Amir didn't say anything. The way he surveyed her made Cassie look away, tension ratcheting up.

'I'm an actress,' she blurted out to fill the silence. 'It's important I keep limber. You'd be surprised how much performing takes out of you.' Besides, with her weakness for sweets, and her tendency to gain weight on the hips just looking at a block of her favourite dark chocolate, she knew the importance of exercise.

'An actress?' One dark brow arched high. 'What do your parents think of that?'

She almost smiled at his reaction to her profession. 'It's a respectable job, you know.' When he didn't respond she shrugged. 'I have no parents. My mother died last year.'

'I'm sorry.' He paused, his brow puckering. 'You must have lost your father young.'

It was on the tip of Cassie's tongue to agree and end the conversation, but looking up into Amir's concerned expression she found the lie died on her lips.

Cassie had spent a lifetime perfecting the art of keeping her private life private, her thoughts a closed book. Yet something about this man with the penetrating eyes had her spilling all sorts of things. Like the night she'd admitted her fears and felt ridiculously comforted by his response.

'My father…' She shrugged and looked over Amir's shoulder. 'We're estranged.' That was a polite way of putting it. He'd never wanted to know about her.

'But he has an obligation to care for you. To protect you.'

Cassie turned away, her movements stiff. She settled herself on a cushion by the low table.

'Cassie?'

She looked up to find him scowling. He'd seemed worn and

tense when he'd arrived, and all she'd done was make things worse.

'It's all right. Really. Water under the bridge.' She reached out and plucked a dried apricot from the earthenware platter a servant had brought.

In a single smooth movement Amir dropped cross-legged beside her. His knee grazed her thigh and she had to force herself not to shuffle away lest he realise how his nearness affected her.

'Tell me.'

Cassie looked at the apricot and knew its sweetness would turn sour in her mouth. She put it on the edge of the platter. 'My father's idea of caring was to pay for me to attend boarding school as early as possible to get me out of the way.'

'Perhaps he sought a good education for you.'

She flashed Amir a hot glance and shook her head. 'He never wanted me. I was an inconvenience. It was easier for him if I wasn't underfoot.'

Silence. Amir reached for the apricot she'd rejected and bit into it. She tried and failed not to let her gaze linger on his strong white teeth, the movement of his jaw. His lips. Were they soft as she imagined?

'Men aren't renowned for showing affection.'

She laughed then. A bitter little chirrup of sound that revealed too much of the hurt she'd thought she'd buried years ago. She snapped her mouth shut.

'Cassie? What is it?'

Cassie tilted her head and met his eyes. They were impossibly dark, yet she could swear she read sympathy there. She felt its impact like a missile blasting apart her carefully constructed defences. In all her years there'd been precious little sympathy or understanding. It wasn't something she expected. It made her feel...vulnerable.

Cassie didn't do vulnerable. Survival depended on being decisive and independent.

That was why she kept herself busy. Always looking for the next challenge, throwing herself into new projects as a way of ignoring the emptiness that threatened. That was how she'd got into teaching drama at a community centre. That in turn had sparked her interest in volunteering abroad.

'It's kind of you to be concerned, but it's all in the past.'

His steady gaze told her he didn't buy that.

She drew a slow breath. 'My parents weren't married. My father already had a family and he had no intention of advertising my presence.'

'I see.'

Cassie doubted it. But she wasn't about to mention the fact that her mother had lived as mistress to Cassie's father for years while he stayed with his wife and legitimate family. Neither had wanted a kid in the way to cramp their style. Cassie had been an encumbrance, an accident that shouldn't have happened.

'So there's no one to worry about my choice of career. I make my own decisions.'

'And who is there now, worrying what's become of you?' Amir's voice, like an undercurrent of silk, cut through her bravado.

She pasted on a bright smile. 'The school I'm going to isn't expecting me for another week. But my landlady's expecting a postcard from Tarakhar, and my girlfriends are looking forward to hearing all about my adventures when I get back. I'll have plenty to tell them, won't I?'

He didn't smile. 'So there's no one special?'

Cassie swallowed. 'No.'

She'd been alone all her life. Why, now, did that suddenly seem so momentous? She blinked, mortified at the emotion welling out of nowhere.

'What about you?' Is there someone waiting at home? Someone special?' It wouldn't surprise her to discover he had a girlfriend patiently waiting. Or perhaps a wife.

Why hadn't she thought of that before? Her stomach plunged into icy distress at the thought she'd shared a bed with a married man, dreamt of him touching her in ways she'd never let any man touch her.

Cassie's stomach churned at the idea of Amir with another woman. That had to be a bad sign, surely?

'No one special.' He didn't smile, just held her eyes with an intensity that made every nerve stir.

Something unspoken lay between them. Something portentous that she couldn't put a name to.

The silence between them stretched beyond companionable. Her pulse beat a quickening tattoo as she tried not to respond to the scent of sandalwood and warm male skin that invaded her nostrils and darted her thoughts in prohibited directions.

She strove for a change of subject, flustered as she hadn't been since that first night.

'Do you enjoy acting?' He came to her rescue, slanting his gaze down at her hands, threading together in her lap.

Instantly Cassie stilled. 'I love it. Most of the time.' Drama had been a refuge and an escape.

'But not always?'

She shrugged. 'Like everything, it's got its ups and downs.' There were too many men who believed actresses, particularly ones who looked like her, were either dumb or easy or both. 'But I make a living…most of the time. I wait tables and do whatever else I have to in order to make ends meet. It took me ages to save up for the fare here.'

'It was so important that you work here as a volunteer?'

'It's something I want to do.' She lifted her shoulders in a casual shrug, unwilling to try explaining the importance of this opportunity. With Amir she found herself revealing too much and this was…private.

Though she loved acting, increasingly she felt a need for something more in her life. Despite the bonhomie she'd found in her profession, there was a focus on individual careers—every man and woman for themselves.

All her life Cassie had felt adrift and alone. Time and again she'd tried to connect with her mother without success. Her mother had blamed Cassie for her break-up with the one man she'd claimed to care for: Cassie's father. Having a kid underfoot, she'd said, had destroyed the romance. After that she'd shut everyone out emotionally—especially Cassie—never displaying anything like true caring again.

Cassie had forged that experience into self-reliance and decisiveness. Yet she yearned for something more solid. Stability, purpose, community. A sense of contributing.

These months in Tarakhar would help her decide if she wanted more permanent changes in her life.

Avoiding Amir's penetrating gaze, Cassie reached for an apricot, inadvertently colliding with him as he leaned forward. Amir jerked violently away as if scalded.

Stunned, Cassie watched his features grow taut, the grooves bracketing his mouth carving deep. A frown pleated his brow as he yanked his hand back from the table.

He looked forbidding, as if she'd trespassed into private territory.

Which she had. He was royalty, used to the best of everything, and here he was sharing his private accommodation with an unwanted guest. A guest who normally would be far beneath his notice.

She waited for him to make some light remark, change the subject and put her at ease as he did so often.

He remained silent.

In a flurry of movement Cassie made to rise.

'Stay!' It wasn't a request. It was a command.

Amir reached out as if to prevent her rising, but his hand halted a telling distance from her arm. As if touching her tainted him. Unbidden, she recalled him holding her behind him as he faced the dangerous mob. His fingers stroking ointment on her bruised skin. Had he felt distaste then at the need for contact?

The look on his face was grimly remote. Vanished was their easy camaraderie. Had she imagined approval in his eyes? Or had it just been a mask for disdain?

It wasn't fair or reasonable, but out of the blue the old sense of inferiority swamped her. Worse this time, because Amir was the catalyst. The man from whom she'd come to expect support.

She'd lost count of the times people had pulled away, distancing themselves when they learned the truth about her parents. About why her father had paid the bills at the elite school where she'd never felt welcome. There'd been the girls who'd made her life hell. The teachers who'd watched her with prurient curiosity or distaste. The parents who'd looked down their noses at her, as if fearing she might contaminate one of their precious darlings.

A lifetime's hurt shuddered to the surface as she looked from his hand into his set face.

Try as she might she could read nothing in his stern expression but rejection and disapproval.

'If you'll excuse me.' She needed all her dramatic skill to keep her voice cool, as if pain didn't cramp her vocal cords and frozen lungs. 'I know when I'm not wanted.'

Cassie scrambled to rise, hampered by the long cloak. She'd rather sit in the bathroom than remain here.

A hand clamped around her wrist and tugged so hard she plopped back down to the cushions, her breath escaping in a whoosh of disbelief.

Amir didn't release her. His long fingers encircled her, firm and warm. Darts of sensation shot through her from his touch and she silently berated herself—because even now she revelled in the feel of his skin against hers.

Cassie stared at him, furious, hurt and, despite herself, curious.

He gave nothing away. His features might have been carved centuries ago, by a sculptor with an eye for beauty and character. Strong nose, purposeful jaw, deeply hooded eyes that hinted at secrets well kept. A mouth that drew her gaze and made her blood rise and effervesce.

'You are.'

Cassie was so absorbed in studying his face, trying to read his thoughts, that the words didn't penetrate.

'Sorry?' With an effort she dragged her reluctant gaze from his lips, over his face of dark gold, to eyes suddenly revealed in blazing glory.

'You are…wanted.'

The words hung between them and it seemed they both held their breath. Nothing moved.

Her brain crashed into gear. That look in his eyes…

Cassie swallowed. Her pulse jumped under his long fingers. She remembered the sensation of his touch, his breath on her bare midriff when he'd worked on that ancient padlock. She felt the hard muscle of his thigh against hers and her mouth dried.

'There's no need to spare my feelings.' Indignation lingered.

His mobile mouth quirked up at one side in an expression that could have signalled wry amusement or possibly pain.

'I'm not given to platitudes, Cassie. I say what I mean.' He drew a breath that expanded his chest mightily. His fingers slid down till he held her hand. 'You are welcome in my tent. *More than welcome.*'

'It's kind of you to—'

'It's not kindness.' His voice was rich and dark like treacle, swirling languidly around her senses. 'I'm not a kind man. I have no experience of it. But I am truthful. Believe me when I say I want you.'

The breath whooshed from Cassie's lungs as she finally allowed herself to read the meaning in his glittering gaze.

Want in the physical, sexual sense.

Want in the way she'd avoided all her life. From the day she'd understood what being a 'kept woman' meant. The day she'd understood her mother survived by pandering to the sexual needs first of Cassie's father and then, when he dumped her, of a string of equally wealthy, demanding men who had precious little respect for her.

Yet, reading the stark hunger in Amir's eyes, feeling the loose grasp of his hand around hers, it wasn't the usual revulsion Cassie felt.

It was a thrill of excitement.

Only days ago the thought of Amir looking at her with desire had made her reach for a knife. But now...

The continual restless undercurrent, the hum of awareness and edginess when she thought of Amir or when he drew near, finally made sense.

For the first time in her life Cassie *wanted*. Wanted a stranger she barely knew. A stranger who'd cared for her with more genuine tenderness than anyone she'd known.

A tremor rippled through her, making her hand shake in his. His fingers wrapped more tightly around hers.

'Don't look so stunned, little one. Is it so surprising? You're a beautiful woman. A fascinating woman.'

His gaze lingered warmly—not on her curves, but her face. Almost as if it was more than her body that appealed.

'I don't... I can't...' Stunned, she shook her head. She was bereft of words. She, the expert at deflecting propositions with a light-hearted quip! Who'd sashayed unscathed past the minefield of sexual relationships with never a backwards glance.

This was different. With Amir for the first time Cassie experienced the compelling desire for intimacy. It was in the gnawing sensation deep in her womb, the need to touch him and snuggle up against his hard body. No wonder she'd been stir crazy these past days! It wasn't just her confinement; it was Amir getting under her skin.

His grip loosened and his fingers slid away. Bereft, she watched his hand bunch on his thigh. She wanted to reach out and stroke him, wrap her hand around his.

'Don't worry, Cassie. You don't have to do anything.'

Her head jerked up and she met his gaze, once more unreadable, all trace of incendiary heat banished. He looked distant, as if that moment of unbridled desire had never been.

'I want you, but you are safe under my protection. Even from me!'

Once more his mouth tilted in that one-sided smile, and this time she'd swear it was pain she read there.

Cassie opened her mouth to blurt out what she felt. That she'd been going slowly mad these past days, trying to battle the uncharacteristic need to be with him. Not just share that wide bed, but share herself.

She shook her head, innate caution intervening. They'd never even kissed, had barely talked, yet the force of her tumultuous feelings was undeniable.

The force of this yearning scared her.

She'd grown up despising her mother's lifestyle, so bitterly cold-hearted beneath the surface gloss. Despising the men who'd used her mother to satisfy their egos and sexual appetites. That had tainted Cassie's dealings with men and she'd never felt anything like this urgent attraction.

It left her floundering, torn between excitement and fear.

Could it be because of their forced proximity? Some strange version of Stockholm Syndrome? Did the danger and isolation make her fancy herself falling for not her kidnapper but the man who would rescue her?

How could she believe what she felt was real?

Yet it felt blood-pulsingly real: urgent and demanding.

She dared to reach out and touch his fist, only to see it turn white-knuckled.

'Don't touch me, Cassie.' At his sharp tone she snatched her hand back. 'This is already a test of willpower. Don't make it more difficult to keep my word.'

He spoke so coolly she was tempted to believe it was all a hoax. That for some reason he played with her, pretending to desire. But, touching him, she'd felt the tension shimmer through him, an unseen vibration.

Amir desired her.

And Cassie wanted him!

Yet surely she'd be a fool to give in to this dangerous desire, no matter how intense, no matter how tempting.

CHAPTER EIGHT

'You're a talented chess player.'

Cassie's face lit with pleasure. Then she looked away hurriedly, as if guilty at enjoying the compliment.

The light flickered in a caress over her lovely features. Cassie grew more vibrant, more engaging, with each hour. It was as if a fire had been lit within her, giving her a glow that drew him like a moth to raw flame.

How was a man to resist?

It should be easy. Though he'd spelled out his desire for her she hadn't reciprocated, hadn't encouraged.

That guaranteed she stayed off-limits. No matter the provocation of too many sleepless nights, his body taut with the need for restraint.

The abduction had made her vulnerable. Was it any wonder she had no interest in pursuing what he guessed would be a combustible passion between them?

He shouldn't have revealed his feelings. Yet her revelations had thrown him off balance. He'd been stunned by the searing hurt he'd felt on her behalf, hearing about her neglectful family and reading the vulnerability behind her bravado.

Amir had grown up distanced from everyone, especially his family. It was that isolation, that need to prove himself against doubts and scorn, that had made him successful and self-sufficient. He'd never had time for regrets. Emotion was something he eschewed.

Yet hearing snippets of Cassie's story something inside

him had cracked. He'd wanted to make someone pay for the distress she tried so valiantly to hide. Comfort her.

As if *he* had experience in providing comfort! Pleasure, yes—that was easy. But he sensed Cassie needed far more.

'I used to play chess a lot.'

'So I can see.'

She collected his rook in a daring move. 'But I'm a bit rusty,' she admitted as he captured her knight.

'Check.'

She nodded and bit her lip, her brow puckering in concentration. Amir wanted to stroke her soft lips, then press his mouth there, taste her sweetness on his tongue.

His grip tightened on the captured knight. Three more days and they'd be out of here. Three more days and he could give Cassie space till she was ready to be persuaded.

For the first time Amir discovered no other woman would do. It was *Cassie* he wanted. Not one of the many women so eager for his attention.

Cassie alone tortured him every hour. Even when he closed his eyes she was there, waiting to tempt him. She was becoming a fixation.

'Who taught you to play?'

She raised her eyes and instantly he was lost in those wary violet depths.

'A teacher at school. The same one who taught me debating and drama.'

'You were busy.'

Her luscious mouth pursed into a sultry bow and she lunged forward, moving a piece seemingly at random.

'I was the poster girl for extracurricular activities.' Her smile was perfunctory. 'I did them all—from badminton to archery, baking, French conversation, a dozen crafts, and later even motor mechanics. I could play the piano and the saxophone before I got to high school, but I had to quit violin to save everyone's ears.'

'A high achiever.' Amir could relate to that.

Again and again they'd given him new tasks to master, new skills they'd been sure he'd fail. He'd forced himself to master them all, to excel, especially at the traditional skills of a Tarakhan warrior. His uncle and the rest had been so certain Amir could never take his place among them. Their contempt had driven him to prove them all wrong.

Cassie shook her head. 'I'd rather have been playing a game or reading a book, but I wasn't given a choice. After-school lessons kept me away from home. Much more convenient than having me underfoot. Then when I was boarding it was easier to keep me occupied rather than pestering to come home.'

Again that shaft of anger mixed with regret and pain speared him. She spoke so matter-of-factly, not lingering in search of sympathy, yet she had it.

What was it about Cassie Denison that made him *feel* so much? Empathise, where in the past he'd had no difficulty retaining a discreet, unbreachable distance from those who, since his accession, wanted to get close?

'How about you? Did your father teach you chess?' She looked up at a point near his ear, then lowered her gaze. He found that almost-collision of eyes infuriating. Unsatisfactory. He wanted…what he couldn't have.

'Hardly.' The word emerged more brusquely than he'd intended and she looked up sharply. 'A palace servant taught me.'

'Really? Like an old family retainer?'

'Something like that. My uncle was horrified that I didn't know the basics of the game when I came to live in Tarakhar. He ordered one of the staff to instruct me.'

'You weren't born in Tarakhar? How did you become Sheikh?' She tilted her head in curiosity, then hurriedly turned to focus on the board.

'The Council of Elders chose me as the most suitable leader from the members of my extended family.' Amir's lips twisted derisively.

How times had changed. Once they wouldn't have given

him the time of day, much less bestowed the nation into his safekeeping.

'What is it?' She peered up at him again, obviously seeing the emotion he usually kept to himself. Why did he find himself letting down his guard with her more and more?

'Nothing. Just that when I came to Tarakhar I wasn't well regarded. I would have been last on the list to be given a public role.'

'Why? What had you done?'

She stirred, and Amir caught her skin's warm fragrance, fresh and tempting. 'I hadn't done anything. I was only eleven.' He watched her brows furrow in that tiny frown she wore when thinking, and repressed the impulse to stroke it away.

He sat straighter.

'I don't understand.'

Clearly Cassie didn't read the gossip columns. Or perhaps it was such old news the press didn't bother to dig up scandalous snippets any more. It had been years since he'd bothered to read what they printed about him.

Amir moved a piece, surprised to find she'd begun to turn the tables and attack.

'My father was youngest brother to the old Sheikh, so I was a member of the ruling family. But we didn't live in Tarakhar.'

'You were raised with your mother's family?'

'Hardly!' There'd been no family at all on his mother's side. His mother hadn't even known who her own father was. On her birth certificate 'unknown' had been inserted instead of a father's name. His uncle had made sure Amir learned that, as well as a lot of other facts he'd have preferred never to know. 'My parents moved around. They didn't have a home but stayed in hotels and resorts. One day the Caribbean, the next, Morocco or the South of France.'

'It sounds exotic.'

He shrugged, feeling a strange tautness in his shoulders. It reminded him of the tension that had gripped him as a kid, when he'd borne the weight of others' expectations—not their hopes, but their certainty he'd fail.

'I suppose it *was* exotic.' He moved a chess piece in a strategy to corner her. 'To me it was just a blur of hotel rooms and unfamiliar faces.' They'd never stayed in one place long enough for him to make friends, and his parents had had a habit of sacking the nannies hired to look after Amir just as he was beginning to know them.

Not that he'd seen much of his parents. They'd had no time for their son. They'd been too engrossed in pursuing the increasingly elusive 'good times' they had lived for.

'Why weren't you well regarded?' Cassie's soft voice tugged him back to the present.

Amir looked into searching eyes and felt a surprising urge to talk. His personal life was a topic he never discussed, even though much of it was on public record.

'I was surrounded by scandal from the moment I was born. No, before I was born.' He watched her move and pretended to survey the board when it was Cassie he wanted to watch. 'My father was the black sheep of the family. You name it, he tried it, from squandering his fortune through gambling to embezzling public funds.'

'You're kidding!'

Amir shook his head. 'He relied on his older brother to bail him out of strife and cover up for him. And he was right—the old Sheikh would have done anything to ensure he didn't face imprisonment. That would have brought shame on the family. In the end my father lived on a very generous stipend provided by his brother.'

'So he could afford the resorts?'

'And more. He was a womanizer, a party animal. The only reason he married my mother was because she was pregnant with his baby.'

'At least he married her.'

Amir watched something flicker in Cassie's eyes and

remembered what she'd said about her parents not being married. About her father living with his other family.

It sounded hard, but if her father had been like his perhaps her experience was the better option.

Slowly he nodded. 'It was the one responsible thing he did in his life. To his family's horror, though, he married a lingerie model with a slum upbringing and a reputation for kiss-and-tell affairs.' His smile was a tight twist of the lips. '*Not* what the Tarakhan royal family had hoped for.'

'I'll bet not.' Cassie sat back, the chessboard forgotten.

'The fact that they died together from an overdose of illegal drugs at an out-of-control party only made things worse.'

'Oh, Amir! I'm so sorry.'

He leaned across to take another of her pieces. He didn't need sympathy. He'd barely known his parents and hadn't missed them. If anything, the move to Tarakhar had been a blessed relief, despite his uncle's rules and regimen.

'It was a long time ago. But the point is when I arrived everyone looked sideways at me. My uncle expected me to turn out like my father—unstable and irresponsible. Everyone else followed his lead.'

'That's *so* unfair!'

'Who said life was fair?' He paused. 'Maybe knowing everyone expected me to fail was what gave me to strength to keep trying. To succeed.'

Amir kept his voice light, but memories reinforced the promise he'd long ago made to himself. No children of his would suffer as he'd done, because of his parents' scandalous behaviour. They wouldn't wear the badge of shame for something they couldn't change.

He would protect them as he'd never been protected. He had it all mapped out. Nothing would be left to chance.

He watched Cassie's slim fingers move a chess piece rather than let himself seek out her gaze.

'Surely your uncle could have given you the benefit of the doubt? You were just a kid.'

'My uncle was a decent man, but after a lifetime bailing his brother out of trouble his patience had worn thin. He spent years waiting for me to show the same traits as my father.'

'But you didn't.'

She said it with such certainty that Amir lifted his gaze to her still face. Something gleamed in the depths of her eyes. Something warm and reassuring. Something that, crazily, for this moment, he wanted to hang on to.

'I'm no saint, Cassie. I haven't always stuck to the straight and narrow.'

Cassie looked away from his dark eyes. They discussed him, yet she felt he saw too much of what she usually kept to herself.

Like the shiver of excitement inside when their eyes met. Like the feeling of connection to this man who was still virtually a stranger.

Yet, hearing about his childhood, she couldn't help but notice the similarities between them. Neither had been wanted as children—definitely in her case, and reading between the lines she'd guess in Amir's as well. Both were children of parents intent on their own pleasure. Both shadowed by the shame of their parents' behaviour. Both ostracised by others because of that.

Both alone.

'I'm not surprised you rebelled. It's a natural response.' She watched him move again, closing the trap around her king.

His movements were mesmerising. Or was it that she'd fallen under his spell? She hung on his words, addicted to the deep timbre of his voice. She watched him move whenever she could, enjoying his lithe grace and athleticism.

She'd bet anything part of his rebellion had been seducing women. Was he a playboy like his father?

Amir had charm when he wanted to exert it, and that dry, self-deprecating humour was far too attractive. Not to mention the sizzle in his eyes when he'd spoken of wanting her. Her pulse revved at the thought.

But most of all it was his aloofness, the sense that he stood alone, that intrigued. It made Cassie want to wrap her arms around him and draw him close. Learn what lay behind that guarded expression and comfort him.

Surely if anything was needed to prove her reaction to him was foolish that was it? As if Amir wanted comfort! She'd never met anyone so self-contained.

Despite what he'd said about desiring her, he'd been nothing but honourable. Protective. A man to rely on.

'Did you rebel too?' His voice came soft and low, feathering across her senses.

'Not so much rebel as escape. Acting was how I got away when things were difficult. I could escape to another world, be who I wanted to be. I could be funny or tragic. I could act out my emotions and blot out what was happening around me.'

'Sounds like it was tough.'

Cassie looked up and found he'd leaned closer, his look intent. Her skin drew tight in a flurry of tingles and she had to concentrate on not gulping in air too fast. When he looked at her like that all she could think of was him saying he wanted her.

It became difficult to remember why she should hold back.

'I got by. I grew strong.'

It took all her willpower to break his gaze and look down at the board. For a moment she couldn't make sense of it, had lost track of the strategy she'd chanced against him. Then, in a moment of clarity, she remembered.

Cassie couldn't prevent the tiny smile that curled her lips as she moved her queen, then looked up into his stunned face. 'Checkmate.'

Cassie stretched voluptuously, in her half-asleep state enjoying the hazy sensation of bone-deep comfort. Had she ever felt this relaxed, this cosy?

She rubbed her cheek against the pillow, warm and cushioned and so slightly abrasive.

Frowning, she pulled herself higher.

Pillows should be soft, shouldn't they?

No matter. This was deliciously warm and—

'Cassie.'

She felt Amir's voice rumble through her. How did he do that?

'Hmm?'

'I think you should move.'

She shook her head, burrowing closer into the spice-scented heat of the bed. She didn't want to move. Didn't want him to talk and wake her fully.

Lying here half dreaming was bliss.

'Cassie.' This time she felt the word like a purr passing through her torso.

'No.' Fretfully she turned her head, clinging to the remnants of sleep. She had nowhere to go, had she? He was the one who left this wonderful bed each morning to go out, leaving her prey to boredom and worry.

'You need to move.'

'Why?' Just a few minutes more. Just—

'Because...' He muttered under his breath and Cassie felt the last vestiges of sleep slide away. 'Because of this.'

Large hands settled on her upper arms and hauled her higher. Startled, she snapped open her mouth to protest, opening her eyes at the same time.

She had a moment's confused impression of a heated black gaze and then something brushed her mouth. Something soft and warm and inviting.

Instantly realisation hit. She was in bed with Amir. Not *in bed*, safely curled on the far side of the wide mattress, but in bed, lying sprawled over him!

It was his bare chest beneath her that generated the heat she'd snuggled into.

His lips slid against hers again in a gentle caress. Her eyes flickered shut as he slipped the tip of his tongue into her mouth in a light foray that made every sense leap.

She clung tight as he thrust further, bringing delight with every slow, lush move of his tongue against hers. Heat coiled inside as rivulets of sensation spread through her, merging and rising into a floodtide of pleasure.

She shouldn't enjoy this. She shouldn't respond. But she did. It was what she'd experienced in those fitful dreams these past few days, and so much more.

With a sigh she sank down into Amir, tilting her head to allow better access to her mouth, answering his kiss with her own demands.

His broad chest was beneath her own, his hot skin bare to her touch. She lay half across him, her right leg on his right, his bunched muscles exciting. The long cotton shirt she wore was no barrier between them. The sensation of skin on skin, of her softness against his hardness, incited a heady thrill she'd never experienced.

He moved, wrapped one arm around her waist, cupped her face in his splay-fingered hand, and she almost moaned her pleasure aloud. His touch was proprietorial and she revelled in it.

Of its own volition her mouth mimicked his, her tongue dipping into his mouth and discovering his delicious taste.

Deeper, deeper the kiss grew. Her senses swirled in heady delight as she fell into the sensuous give and take.

Cassie had been kissed before. On stage she'd scored more than her fair share of kisses, from quick pecks to lavish seductions. Away from the stage there'd been men too. Some she'd even encouraged as she'd tried to shake off her fears and her ingrained distaste. But it had never worked. No one had broken through the mental barriers she'd erected and strengthened with every passing year.

Those barriers had kept her from giving herself to a man. No one had ever swept her away on a wave of pleasure till her mind refused to engage and all she could do was feel. Until now.

Amir's taste, spicy and dark and male, filled her senses. It mingled with the fresh, clean scent of his skin. Not like hers but intriguingly different and desirable. Unique.

His touch was tender but his body was hard, inciting a terrible longing that made Cassie shift restlessly and lean closer.

His hand moved up, threading through her hair, and she thought she'd die of pleasure. It was a massage so seductive, attuned to the deepening rhythm of their kiss and the rising need within her.

Cassie wanted more. She spread her hands over Amir's shoulders, stroking the hot silk of his skin over rigid muscle and bone. She lifted a hand to his jaw, fascinated by the tiny abrasive film of stubble that felt so satisfyingly rough to her palm and tickled the corner of her mouth.

He shifted and the friction of his solid chest against her breasts notched tension within her. An urgency built, making her move fretfully, demanding more.

Amir gave it. In a single surge he gripped her close and rolled her onto her back. Cassie revelled in the sense of him propped half over her, blanketing out the world. His mouth worked magic, making her head spin.

His hand strayed to her jaw, her throat, and a delicate shudder ripped through her at his butterfly-light caress.

Her heart hammered to a new, urgent tattoo as she willed his hand lower, for the first time wanting, *needing* a man's touch on her breast.

Her skin tingled and her blood roared. Deep inside something loosened: a tightness, a constriction she'd never noticed. Cassie felt free, wonderfully alive, breathless with anticipation.

'Please,' she whispered against his mouth, hardly knowing what she wanted except that it was *more*.

A moment later his warm hand cupped her breast. Delicious heat shot through her. She moved restlessly and his hold tightened. A deep growl of masculine pleasure vibrated through her and he shifted his weight.

His fingers flexed again, but this time Cassie felt no pleasure, only a sudden suffocating fog.

A flutter of unease stirred and her eyes snapped open. He loomed huge above her in the half-dark.

The tantalising pleasure of Amir's kiss bled away. In its place erupted choking fear.

She was helpless against the strength of this big, powerful man. Abruptly, from the depths of her subconscious, came the memory of being pinioned to a door, fondled by the man who'd just emerged from her mother's bedroom. She could almost hear his hoarse chuckle as she writhed in his hold.

Somehow the hot, clean scent of Amir's skin was obliterated by the sour tang of sweat, wine and musky aftershave.

Bile rose and Cassie's stomach cramped in fear.

She had to get out, draw breath. But she couldn't break his hold.

A sob of terror rose in her throat as she shoved at those rigid shoulders. She kicked fruitlessly, hampered by the unyielding form above her.

Suddenly she was free. She scrambled to the far side of the bed, gasping desperate breaths as she pulled her knees high and wrapped her arms around them.

Finally, when the miasma lifted, she turned her head. Amir sat hunched on the other side of the bed, one hand thrust through his crisp dark hair. His shoulders rose and fell as he dragged in deep breaths and she spied tiny crimson marks there. Scratches where she'd dug her nails in as she'd frantically tried to shift him.

Cassie's breath froze.

What had happened? One moment she'd been eager for Amir. The next, claustrophobic fear had risen and flung her into panicked resistance.

'Are you all right?'

He'd swung round. Dark eyes full of concern held hers.

Silently she nodded, unable to find her voice.

She trembled all over, suddenly cold though seconds ago she'd been burning with desire and the heat of Amir's body against hers.

'I…' His hand slashed through the air—in a gesture of frustration or anger? She couldn't tell. 'Don't look at me like that, Cassie!'

He surged to his feet and strode across the dimly lit room away from her. A moment later he'd grabbed a long cloak and whirled it round his shoulders.

When he turned his face was set like stone, though his eyes held a febrile glitter.

'I apologise.' He took half a step towards her then stopped. 'That won't happen again. I thought you wanted—' He shook his head. 'You are safe.'

Guilt rose in Cassie. She *had* wanted. She'd wanted so badly.

'It's not your fault.' Her voice emerged husky from her constricted throat. 'I…'

The words died as he turned away, the cloak flaring around him.

'Sleep now, Cassie. No one will disturb you.' Then he marched from the room, barefoot but impossibly regal.

Cassie was left alone with her thoughts.

She'd never craved company more.

CHAPTER NINE

GRAVEL bit into his bare feet as he stalked across the dawn-lit compound but Amir barely registered the pain.

Instead it was the recollection of Cassie's fear that gripped him. The glazed horror in her eyes when he'd broken their kiss had shocked him.

How had he got it so wrong?

Yes, she'd been barely awake when he'd tried to make her move.

Yes, he'd been aroused, and all too ready to let his body do the thinking as he'd lain, tormented, beneath her sumptuously feminine body.

Yes, he'd known he shouldn't, but he'd been unable to resist kissing her, deepening the kiss as she'd responded.

He'd read her plea as an invitation to pleasure, believing she felt the same simmering desire that had short-circuited his brain. He'd deluded himself into thinking she wanted him as much as he wanted her.

How had he not heard instantly the desperation in her voice? How had he misinterpreted what must have been a plea for escape as a throaty-voiced request for seduction?

Bitter recriminations filled his head and guilt slashed a jagged slice through his belly.

He reached an outcrop of bare rock on the edge of camp and stood, watching the fingers of dawn light spread down from the mountain towards Tarakhar.

If only they were there now. Cassie would be cared for and

comfortable as she recuperated from her ordeals. She wouldn't have to share accommodation with a man who, despite his vaunted control, had almost taken far more than he should have.

Amir was sick to his stomach at the thought of what he'd almost done.

He recalled Cassie's desperation that first night. The fear in her voice as she'd related how she'd expected to be assaulted at any moment. How he'd reassured her she was safe with him.

A bitter laugh escaped him.

Safe?

The horror in her wide eyes moments ago told its own tale.

Two more days till their scheduled departure. Two days during which she'd fear he'd make a move on her. Two days in which he wouldn't sleep for fear of waking again to a situation he couldn't control.

He couldn't do it.

He swung round and strode back across the camp. With a supreme effort he might just be able to finalise the work he'd come here to do in one day. Then they'd only have one night to get through. Surely one more night was possible?

Cassie lay in the massive bed, unable to sleep.

She hadn't seen Amir since dawn.

Now she heard laughter and music on the night air. There must be a feast in the main tent tonight. As guest of honour Amir would attend.

Why did it hurt so much that he'd avoided her all day?

She was frantic to explain he wasn't to blame. To wipe away the guilt she'd read on his face as he'd looked at her with shock pinching his features.

The soft brush of his lips had been an invitation to pleasure, not a demand. It had been *her* plea for more that had galvanised him into action, as she'd thought she wanted.

Cassie pummelled the pillow. She needed to explain. She needed…

Cassie shied from the thought filling her head. Yet it wouldn't disappear. She knew what she *wanted*.

She wanted Amir.

Wanted him as she'd never wanted any man.

For days she'd tried to convince herself what she felt was an aberration caused by their bizarre circumstances. That, once she was free of this place, he'd lose his allure.

It wasn't true. She'd been too scared to face the truth.

Why shouldn't she desire him? He was strong, handsome and honourable. He respected her.

Then she forced herself to face another truth.

Her reaction this morning had been anything but normal. She'd wanted Amir, begged him for more. And when he'd obliged she'd frozen with terror at the memory of something that had happened in her teens.

Curtis Bevan hadn't raped her all those years ago. But he'd made her feel unclean, tainted by his touch and his lascivious intentions. After that she'd been only too glad to return to boarding school, away from the man who thought that paying for her mother gave him rights to Cassie too.

Now she glimpsed the possibility that that event, coupled with the stigma of her mother's way of life, had affected her more than she'd thought.

Was she celibate because she hadn't met the right man? Or had her emotional scars made her afraid to give herself?

Cassie had thought herself a survivor. She'd withstood bullying and ostracism. She'd been strong in the face of her mother's neglect and occasional vitriolic outbursts, her father's avoidance. She'd carved a career through talent and hard work.

Cassie had scrimped and saved to make this trip even when supporting herself was a struggle.

When her mother died Cassie had given away her few valuables rather than accept anything bought by her mother's keepers. Even the diamond brooch of which her mum had been so proud. How powerful Cassie had felt donating it to a charity shop, walking out through the door into the sunshine and feeling free of her mother's murky past.

But she wasn't free.

And she wanted to be. As much as she wanted Amir.

It was past midnight when Amir entered the sleeping chamber. He'd stayed as late as possible, though the entertainment hadn't been to his taste. Yet a lamp burned, bathing the wide bed in golden light.

His gaze was riveted on the still form there, her blonde hair flaring on the pillow.

She was asleep. He wouldn't have to face her anxiety.

Nevertheless, he didn't trust himself to sleep with her. Not after that taste this morning had awakened such hunger. He could recall it now: the flavour of her ripe lips, the scent of her honeyed skin, the need he hadn't been able to stop.

A tremor ripped through him and he clenched his hands.

He'd take the floor instead.

Quickly he disrobed and shoved his legs into light trousers. He hefted a bracing breath and reached for a pillow.

'Don't go.'

He froze, pillow in hand, as Cassie broke the silence. He whipped his head around to find her violet gaze on him. Instantly heat shimmered through him, an unholy combination of lust and remorse.

He straightened abruptly. 'I didn't mean to wake you.'

'You didn't.'

Of course she hadn't been asleep. She was probably a bundle of nerves, anxious about sharing that bed.

'Don't worry.' His attempt at a reassuring smile felt tight. 'I'll take the floor tonight.'

'That's not necessary.' She propped herself on one elbow and the covers slid down a fraction.

Amir didn't let his eyes drop to the shadow of her cleavage visible through the slit neck of his shirt. Yet every cell throbbed with awareness.

'It's better this way.' He turned from the bed, loosening his watch. A man knew his limits and Amir had reached his!

'No, Amir.'

Startled, he turned slowly.

Her face was flushed and her eyes glittered with an expression he couldn't read.

'I want to sleep with you,' she said, a defiant note in her voice.

His body locked down as shock and desire tensed every muscle. He couldn't be hearing what he thought he heard. He shook his head.

'I'm sorry about this morning—'

He raised one hand. 'You have nothing to apologise for.'

'But I do.' Cassie sat higher, her hair tumbling round her shoulders like a glossy invitation to touch. 'You did nothing wrong. I wanted your kiss. I wanted more.'

Her eyes dipped and she drew an unsteady breath. Despite his best intentions Amir was transfixed by the sight of her unbound breasts rising tremulously against the fine fabric of his shirt. Her nipples peaked as he watched.

Heat poured over him. He clamped the pillow close to cover his arousal.

'You changed your mind. That's all right.' Amir lifted his shoulders in a gesture of dismissal, but the movement was jerky and uncoordinated, as if his body didn't function properly.

Determined to end this difficult conversation, he wrenched off his watch and reached over to put it on the bedside table.

The expensive timepiece fell from suddenly nerveless fingers with a clunk onto the inlaid surface.

'I didn't think you'd mind.' Cassie's words were rushed, slightly breathless. 'I noticed them in your toiletries bag when I borrowed your comb.'

His eyes rounded in disbelief as he surveyed 'them'.

A neatly stacked pile of condoms.

Amir's heartbeat took up a new rhythm, like the gallop of

hooves across the desert. He stared, and still the sight didn't make sense. He carried condoms like he carried soap or toothpaste. They'd stayed in the bag since his last trip. He certainly hadn't expected to use them here.

'Say something, Amir.'

Say what? That he couldn't trust himself to stop if she changed her mind again? That he was a man of flesh and blood and all too real appetites?

'This is a mistake, Cassie. You were terrified this morning.'

He turned to find she'd edged closer, her eyes solemn and huge. Then he made the mistake of looking at her mouth, the way her lips were parted as if in expectation, the sultry shape of them beckoning.

'It wasn't you. It was just that I suddenly remembered...'

'I can guess.' It must have been terrifying, the sense of helplessness when she'd been abducted. 'But sex with me isn't a cure for your fears.'

He couldn't believe he was talking her out of this!

In dealing with women Amir's allegiance had always been to Amir. Though he'd never consciously harm any woman, self-interest had always dictated his dealings.

Cassie was different. Vulnerable, yet so feisty and determined. He couldn't help but be drawn to her, and want to protect her.

'You know nothing about my fears!' Typically, her chin angled high as she held his eyes, and he was struck again by the fierce independence in her. That strength of character drew him as much as her luscious body.

'In the morning you'll be relieved that we haven't—'

'I won't!' Her voice was strident. 'I know what I want, Amir, even if I didn't this morning. I want you.'

How many times had Amir heard those words, or others like them? How many times had women, silk-clad sirens or glamorous sophisticates, invited him to share their bed? Too many to count. Yet never before had he sensed the raw honesty he saw in Cassie's eyes.

There was a gravity about her, a consciousness of herself and of him, that for a moment locked any words in his throat.

She had such pride, such passion!

And he wanted her so very badly.

His grip tightened on the pillow as he turned away. It was the hardest thing he'd ever done, rejecting Cassie, but he couldn't risk her changing her mind again. Clearly the kidnap still traumatised her. She probably didn't know what she wanted. And if she pulled back from him again he didn't know he had the strength to stop.

'Don't tempt me, Cassie.'

A small hand touched the back of his, lightly, but it was enough to stop him stepping away.

'I *want* to tempt you. Don't you understand? This isn't like this morning. I know what I'm doing.'

Her fingers slid up to his wrist, delicately caressing, and he shuddered. It was all he could do not to move when his inner self screamed for him to pull her to him and finish what they'd begun this morning.

Before he could stop her she'd pulled the pillow from his slackening grip.

He watched as she looked down and caught her breath. She blinked, and her mouth rounded in an O of surprise that impossibly made him harden more.

He really had a thing for those sultry lips. Fire threaded his veins and exploded in his belly as he envisaged those lips on his body.

'You *do* want me.'

'Of course I want you!' Wasn't that the point? He wanted her too much to keep control.

Her mouth curved in the tiniest of satisfied smiles. An instant later she crossed her arms and tugged off the shirt she'd been wearing.

He was lost.

Strong as he was, no power on earth could save him now. Or her.

Amir swallowed hard, his throat dry as the arid mountains, his gaze anchored by her breasts.

In her dancer's clothes she'd looked voluptuous, but it was surprising how much the satin had concealed. The natural tip-tilted lushness of firm breasts. The delicate rosy hue of nipples that puckered invitingly.

Amir's palms itched with the need to touch. He longed to taste and savour.

A low groan filled his chest and spilled into the hushed silence. He stepped up to the edge of the bed and ripped back the covers.

Only the sight of her, fully uncovered, made him pause long enough to enjoy the view. Now he saw not only Cassie's breasts, but her pale thighs, the inviting arc of her hips...

He eyed the dip of her waist where the hated slave chain glinted. Yet this time, in a flash of unrepentant masculine possessiveness, exhilaration sparked at the way it accentuated her feminine shape. At the way it signified she was *his* to possess.

A moment later he was in the bed, drawing her to him.

She came easily, sliding against him in a flurry of soft flesh so tantalising he almost winced at the pleasure of it. Pleasure so intense it bordered on pain.

Unerringly his lips caught hers, his hands slid over her pale, silken skin, learning texture and shape. He gathered her close, breast to chest, and the exquisite rightness of Cassie in his arms stole his breath.

This time her mouth was as hungry as his, urgent as she shaped her lips to him, sucked his tongue in deep and clamped his head between her hands.

She trembled all over, a tiny, delicate tremor that made his chest lurch in a tumble of rare emotion.

Amir forced his hands to slow as they swept her shoulders and back, replacing urgency with a weighted, deliberate caress. Cassie arched into him. Her budded nipples grazed him and sent blood rushing low.

He hooked one leg over hers, holding her in place against

him, and pushed his hips forward. The sensuous pleasure of her soft belly, the feel of skin on skin, shot stars through his vision.

'You're certain?' he groaned, forcing himself to break the kiss and pull back enough to look at her.

He wanted to smile at the dazed delight he read in her eyes.

Even now he wasn't sure he could release her if he needed to.

Her palm slid over his cheek, past his chin, to skim in the lightest of caresses over his throat. He swallowed convulsively as her hand moved further, to flatten and swirl over his chest.

'Absolutely certain.' Her eyes were serious, almost grave, but her lips were plump and soft from his kiss. Her smile was the sweetest he'd ever seen. 'Let me help you.'

She pushed his shoulder till he lay on his back and she leaned over, reaching for the side table. Her breasts brushed him teasingly, her legs slid against his, and the heat at the apex of her thighs warmed him.

'Don't!'

Startled, she stared down into what he guessed was a face full of pain. He wanted Cassie so badly each casual touch was like an incendiary flare, burning his needy body.

How would he last long enough to get a condom fitted if it was Cassie rolling it on him?

Amir gritted his teeth and nudged her backwards.

'I'll do this.'

Without waiting for a response he rolled over, stripped open a packet and sheathed himself.

He turned back, hauled her close and kissed her till he was lost in her heady sweetness and control was a fragile filament. His pelvis rocked hard against her, mimicking the thrust of his tongue in her mouth.

To his delight Cassie curved her body against his, aligning herself to his movements and clutching at him as if she'd never let go.

Amir traced the line of her ribs, rejoicing in her telltale

shiver as he cupped one pouting breast. It was the perfect size for his hand. Gently he swiped his thumb over her nipple and was rewarded with a gasp of shocked pleasure. He did it again, and her whole body bowed back as she pushed her breast deeper into his hold.

He smiled, relieved and delighted at her responsiveness. A moment later he slid down her body, rubbing his cheek against her breast.

Cassie's arms coiled tight round his head, holding him to her. He looked up, caught a flash of wonder in those eyes that had darkened now to indigo. For a moment he could almost believe this was a new experience for her, despite her offer to fit the condom.

Then he ceased thinking as he took her nipple in his mouth and sucked hard, feeling her legs wrap round him in an urgent lock that sent blood roaring through him in a cataclysmic tide.

He wanted. How he wanted.

And so did she.

Amir slipped his hand between their bodies till he zeroed in on the centre of her desire. She was hot and wet, moving urgently at his touch.

Dimly he thought about the need for foreplay. About the need to ensure Cassie's pleasure before his own. But his years of experience fell silent before the compulsion to make her his. Now.

He surged higher, pausing only to bestow a lingering kiss on her other breast, letting it turn into a tiny nip that made the breath hiss between her lips and her hips buck needily.

Then Amir was over her, propped on his elbows. Her eyes held his and there was no spark of fear. Their bodies met and slid together, eager for completion.

Using his knee, Amir nudged one leg aside, then the other. He moved, shifting his weight carefully, to settle in the cradle of her hips.

Was that a flicker of doubt in Cassie's eyes? A shadow?

Amir paused, his breath thundering in his lungs, fists clenched so hard his fingers grew numb from the pressure.

She couldn't say no. He'd die if she did.

But the size and weight of him over her must reinforce her latent fears. Was that what had gone wrong this morning?

Instinct more than reason had him rolling to his side, tugging her with him till he lay on his back with her above him.

'Kiss me,' he ordered, before she had time to think.

Their mouths melded and this time Cassie set the pace, her lips demanding and hungry. Her hands were restless on his face and shoulders, and she shifted against him as if wanting more but not knowing how to get it.

He smoothed his hands down her back, past the chain at her waist, up the curve to her firm buttocks. Slipping further, he took the backs of her thighs in his hands and pulled them wide, so her body opened over his, her knees planted on either side of him.

Yes!

Amir rocked beneath her, exultant at the sensation of flesh against flesh.

Cassie lifted her head, her lips open in a gasp of what he hoped was approval. When she showed no inclination to move he grasped her shoulders.

'Sit up, Cassie. Yes, like that!' The words ended on a deep groan of approval as she slid over the full length of his erection, drawing every nerve to aching arousal.

The sight of her above him, breasts swaying, lips curved in an answering smile, excited him as never before.

With one swift movement he grabbed her hips, lifted her high and centred her over him. His eyelids flickered in anticipated ecstasy at the feel of her heat all around him.

He pulled, slow yet firm, and she slid down, opening for him.

She sheathed him so tightly, so perfectly, it took a moment for him to realise she'd stopped and held herself rigid above him. He felt the muscles in her thighs stiffen, her fingers tighten on his shoulders. Through the rough beat of blood in his ears he thought he heard a gasp. Of discomfort?

'Cassie? Am I hurting you?' She was far smaller than he, and the sensation of pressure around him was intense. For him that meant pleasure, but for her...

'I'm fine.' She blinked and drew a deep breath, then looked down at his torso, as if absorbing every detail for later consideration. A tremor rippled through her legs. Tension or delight? 'It's just...'

'It's been a while?' Amir lifted his hands and smoothed them up her arms, trying to stroke away the tension he felt within her.

'Something like that.'

Fighting the primitive urge to drag her down the rest of the way, he let his hands move to her breasts, lazily cupping and sliding, circling and massaging.

Cassie's head lolled back and he felt her muscles relax as she grew languid under his touch. Her fingers softened against him and he risked a single tiny thrust.

She slid lower, enveloping him in a wall of heat. Another thrust and she moved with him, till finally they were one.

It was everything he'd expected. More.

With her head thrown back she was the image of wanton abandon. His hands moulding her pale breasts was the most erotic thing he'd ever seen. Unless it was the way her lips parted in a soundless sigh as she moved.

She drew out sensations of such exquisite pleasure Amir felt himself sweeping towards ecstasy.

His hands slid down, past the links at her waist, to anchor on her hips. His fingers gripped her smooth flesh, holding her steady as he bucked up, his movements more and more urgent.

Her eyes snapped open and indigo fire burned his retinas as she held his gaze.

Something sizzled through him at her look—something more than the seductive friction of two bodies moving together in harmony and complete abandon.

A wave of pleasure hit him, rolling through him to circle tighter and tighter. Incredulous, he realised there was no time for more, that the climax was upon him.

Amir had opened his mouth to apologise when it took him, racking his body in pleasure so intense he almost blacked out. A galaxy of stars whirled around him, but none eclipsed her deep blue eyes. They held him as he gasped for breath, groaning his ecstasy, shuddering as his body pumped its climax and he held her as if he'd never let her go.

CHAPTER TEN

CASSIE clung on tight as Amir heaved and rocked beneath her. Her untutored body began to respond with tiny ripples of pleasure.

Fascinated, she watched him lose control, as if plucked up by a force of nature and set spinning on another plane.

Excitement had escalated after the initial shock. When he'd touched her breasts that lovely melting sensation had filled her again, like chocolate swirled with cream and her favourite liqueur, and her body had softened around him.

Now the delicious feel of them moving together abated, and with it the tiny thrills that had begun spreading through her. Amir lay unmoving but for the way his chest rose and fell like bellows pumping. He was lax except for the hands that gripped her.

Tentatively she moved. He groaned and clamped her hips into stillness. 'Not yet,' he gasped.

Seconds ticked by and Cassie began to feel the strain where her thighs stretched, feel the little flurries of chill night air around her naked body. Began to feel...exposed, sitting above Amir who, eyes closed, seemed lost in another world.

A world she'd been denied entry to.

With a sudden movement he rolled, tipped her gently onto her side. A moment later he withdrew, and Cassie clamped her lips on the protest that welled as sensitive nerve endings stirred anew. She wanted—

He didn't even look at her, simply turned away, got up and strode to the bathroom.

Helplessly Cassie watched the play of light and shadow on his naked back, the lithe grace of his powerful body, and wished he didn't still take her breath away.

She felt…cheated. After the gloriously intense pleasure of their coupling, surely she'd been right to expect more.

Cassie grimaced and rolled away, pulling the covers high as she slid to her own side of the bed. What had made her think Amir different? Of course he'd put his own pleasure first. If she hadn't quite reached the pinnacle of ecstasy he had, then that, apparently, wasn't his problem.

But he hadn't even *looked* at her! Amir had avoided her eyes as he'd disengaged himself and hurried away. Almost as if he was ashamed of her.

Perhaps he was, now he'd taken what he wanted.

Sly dark shadows stirred, and Cassie felt the murky undercurrents of the past reaching out to her. She felt the tug of shame and anger, and a guilt she couldn't do anything to assuage. Emotions she'd carried all her life.

No! She wasn't her mother. Amir had no right to make her feel tainted.

Or was it Cassie herself making her feel that way?

She clutched a pillow close and set her jaw. At least there was a bright side. For all the disappointment, she'd managed to break through the frozen terror that had filled her earlier at the idea of intimacy. She'd learned it could be electrifying, exhilarating, wonderful! Surely by this act she'd managed to begin healing part of the unseen hurt she'd carried too long?

Next time she'd make sure she chose a man who wouldn't turn his back on her the moment he had what he wanted.

'Cassie?' His breath hazed her neck, and heat surrounded her as he slid naked behind her.

She started, and her breath seized as his arm roped her waist, pulling her towards him so his hair-roughened thighs cradled her and his solid form pressed close.

Every nerve ending shuddered into awareness and the curl of excitement in her womb twisted into life. It wasn't fair! She was angry and disappointed, yet her body betrayed her with its eagerness.

She stiffened and tried to pull away, but he held her. Temper rose at how easily he controlled her.

'I'm sorry, Cassie.' His breath on her ear made her shiver as tendrils of sensation unfurled and spread. 'I couldn't help it. I lost control.'

Dimly she wondered how often that was used by men as an excuse for selfishness.

'You're angry.'

'I—' She shrugged. Maybe her anger was out of proportion with the situation. This was her first experience of sex, and she had a horrible suspicion she was letting the past colour her judgement. 'I didn't like it when you turned away from me like that.'

It had made her feel cheap.

His hand on her shoulder pulled her round till she lay on her back. His face loomed above her like that of a reverently carved idol: beautiful yet remote. His eyes were dark as night and equally impenetrable.

He trailed his fingertips over her collarbone, up her throat to clasp her jaw. The air left Cassie's lungs in a whoosh at the implicit intimacy of his touch.

'I apologise, Cassie. It's a long time since I've had so little control.' Was that the hint of a blush colouring the high angles of his cheekbones?

Cassie frowned, trying to read his precise meaning. 'You were embarrassed?'

His mouth firmed, and if anything his sculpted face grew tauter. 'Only raw youths and selfish lovers take without giving. A certain amount of control is necessary.'

Her eyes widened. Had Amir stepped from a world completely different from the one she'd known? She'd misread him. Instead of casual thoughtlessness, he'd been too ashamed to meet her eyes.

The novel idea stunned her.

'You have a real problem with losing control.'

Amir's eyes glinted and his hand slid tantalisingly low over her breast. 'That makes two of us. I've never met a more fiercely independent woman in my life.'

Cassie gasped as trailing fingers circled her nipple. Dormant pleasure burgeoned. She wanted to savour his words, but instead it was his cheeky caress, now plucking at one rosy tip, that filled her thoughts.

'I—'

'Yes, Cassandra?' This time when he drawled all three syllables of her name in that deep, knowing voice it sounded perfect.

His hand moved lower and she opened her mouth to protest—till she felt his fingers tickle the soft hair between her legs.

'You wanted to say something?'

He didn't smile, but the glint in his eyes told her he knew what effect he had on her.

Sensation hummed through her, coalescing in a single powerful shock of pleasure when he touched her just so.

Amir watched her closely, as if able to gauge what she felt by the blush searing her cheeks and throat. Now it was her turn to feel embarrassed. She wasn't the subject of some scientific study!

Desperately she reached up and hauled his head down, kissing him open-mouthed as he touched her again. This time the bolt of power ignited ecstasy and sent it reverberating through her body. All she knew was his mouth, tender on hers, his touch, and the shock of delight as her whole body turned into a conflagration of scintillating sparks and fiery explosions.

Her hands shook as she held him. She gasped for air but refused to break the kiss that plastered him to her. She wanted to cradle him closer, hold this magic for as long as she could. Hold *him* till she came back to earth.

But Amir had other ideas. Already he was pulling back, easing out of her grasp.

'That hardly touched the surface, did it, *habibti*? You're wound far too tight.' His mouth lifted at one corner in that sexy, wry smile of his, and Cassie's heart shimmied. 'And I still have to make up for my clumsiness before.'

Cassie swiped her tongue across her lips, ready to tell him that, far from being wound tight, she felt totally unravelled.

She didn't even get the first syllable out. Amir dipped his head and took her mouth in a slow kiss that drew deep, demanding a response. It came from a part of her she'd never known existed. A part of her that responded to every nuance of his caress, to each sure stroke of his hand over her throat, her shoulder, breast and hip.

Time and her thoughts blurred as Amir made love to her with his hands, his mouth, his whole body. He evoked slow, lush pleasure. He led her into another intense climax that shattered her soul into thousands of shards. Then he put her back together again with tender caresses and murmured endearments.

She never known such gentleness.

She felt…different. Born anew.

Cassie lay spent, gasping in air, her mind awhirl. This felt like something more than physical. But how could that be?

Through the haze of jumbled thoughts and sensations she felt him move. Heard a tiny sound and opened her eyes to find him tearing open a small square package with his teeth.

She was exhausted, too spent to move, her limbs weighted in the aftershock of bliss. She couldn't possibly want him now in this exhausted state, but she *did* want to hold him close, feel his heart beat next to hers.

Through slitted eyes she watched him roll on protection with dextrous movements. This was a man with lots of experience. In that moment, sated and revelling in the results of his loving, Cassie was glad. At least one of them knew what they were doing.

Nevertheless a tingle of anxiety tripped through her as he knelt between her legs.

She couldn't imagine giving or receiving any more pleasure. But the gleam in his eyes was unmistakable, as was the taut energy in his muscled frame and the erection straining towards her.

'I'm not sure I can.' Even speaking seemed too much effort.

Amir leaned close, his mouth whisper-soft on hers. 'You don't need to do anything. Trust me.'

Dazed, she watched him rise above her, his imposing shoulders blotting out the room. Yet it wasn't trepidation Cassie felt this time, only a sense of rightness.

He moved and her arms came around him, hugging him close as he surged with one easy thrust deep inside.

Home.

That was the word that spun in her brain as he lifted her knee a little, easing his way, then gathered her close.

She was enfolded, blanketed and at peace.

Amir tilted his hips and began a rhythm that was easy, gentle. The give and take lulled Cassie and a smile played about her lips.

'You feel good.'

'So do you.' He kissed her fluttering eyelids and cheeks, then her mouth. He stroked his tongue along the seam of her lips and a tremor of awareness passed through her.

Cassie's eyes popped open.

He cupped her breast, stroked her nipple in a slow arc and something tightened in her belly.

'You know what you're doing.' Her voice was husky.

He dipped his head and favoured her with a long kiss that left her pulse racing. Out of nowhere adrenalin charged through her lax body.

'And you're still in control,' she added.

'Do you mind?' One black eyebrow arched devilishly as he pushed higher, cupped her breast a fraction tighter.

Cassie caught her lip between her teeth in a gasp of surprise and delight.

Somehow she found enough energy to speak. 'No.' Her hands slid to his buttocks, tight and gloriously rounded, and pulled him higher. The resulting sensation almost knocked the breath from her lungs. She lifted her knees, feeling each measured thrust more deeply. 'You won't be for much longer.'

Then she gave in to the desire to taste him. Following instinct, she bit gently on the curve of straining flesh where his neck joined his shoulder.

A shudder ripped through Amir and his movements grew sharper. Suddenly Cassie was no longer teasing. Her body echoed his movements, maximising their impact as he took them both to unbearable heights.

What had started as a lazy game became a headlong rush towards completion. It overwhelmed them both. So sudden, so intense. It was fierce and fulfilling and indescribably wonderful for being shared.

Amir. His name was a shout of ecstasy. An exultation and a plea. Whether she called his name out loud Cassie didn't know, but his name was in every pounding beat of her blood, in each spasm of pleasure and every gasped breath. It was as if she'd absorbed him into herself, become one with him not just bodily but at some deeper level.

The last thing she remembered was Amir holding her tight, rolling onto his back so she sprawled across him.

His breath was hot on her face. His arms held her safe against the cataclysmic force that buffeted them. The sure rhythm of his heart was beneath her ear. It lulled her till exhaustion claimed her.

Dawn. From outside came the sound of the camp stirring: a shout, a jingle of harness. Amir surfaced from the soundest sleep he could recall. Sound and satisfying.

Almost as satisfying as the woman in his arms. She was a bundle of delight. Lushly curved instead of emaciated-chic. Warm, responsive and surprisingly addictive.

Cassie approached sex with wholehearted enthusiasm, as if it were a wondrous new world to explore. Not a battlefield where favours were traded for gifts or prestige or for more of Amir than he chose to give.

She met him as an equal. Asked for nothing save shared pleasure. There was something innately honest about her. Something that snagged his interest in ways other than the physical.

Right now it was the physical that interested him. With her body pressed close she was one hundred percent temptation. He stroked a possessive hand over her.

Still she slept. Could she really be so deeply asleep? There was a clatter outside but she didn't twitch. Did she feign sleep to tempt him to rouse her?

He *was* tempted. He grabbed the covers to slide them off her shoulders, then stopped.

A smear of blood stained the sheet.

Amir frowned. Where was it from? Neither he nor Cassie was injured.

He could have sworn this top sheet had been pushed way down the bed. Hadn't it been under their hips? It couldn't have been. There was only one explanation. Cassie had scored him with her nails.

He smiled. There was an untamed element to Cassie when roused. He couldn't wait to experience it again.

Last night *had* been intense. Witness the way Cassie had clawed at him, and those mind-numbingly powerful climaxes. She was dead to the world—unlike earlier nights when she'd slept restlessly, disturbed by dreams.

His hand slipped from the covers and away from the heat of her body.

Only with Cassie did Amir refrain from initiating sex when

he wanted it. In the past, to desire had been to act. To act had been to satisfy.

After what they'd shared he knew she'd welcome his touch. Yet he restrained himself. There was a strange satisfaction in putting Cassie's needs before his own. He stroked a lock of hair from her face. Watching her curled trustingly close, an unfamiliar peace filled him.

For the first time since boyhood he almost regretted that life had made him a loner. That he'd never had an intimate relationship except on the physical level. For a fleeting moment he experienced something like that old boyhood yearning to *belong* to someone, to be special to someone and have someone special to care for.

As a child it had been a secret craving, hidden deep in the belief that such emotion made him weak when he had to be strong to survive. As a man such sentimentality had no place in his world.

Now he wondered if there could be more in his life.

He shook his head, clearing it of half-formed imaginings.

Yes, he'd marry. Arrangements were already in progress. But, while his bride would provide comfort and pleasure, this would be no love match. No partnership based on attraction or volatile emotions. As a kid he'd learnt what an unstable foundation that was.

He'd marry to ensure a line of inheritance. For the stability of his nation. To shore up the prestige and reputation of his dynasty after so much notoriety and disharmony. His bride had been chosen for her impeccable breeding, her connection to one of the wealthiest, most powerful families in Tarakhar, as well as for her beauty and docility.

Not for him a wife who, like his mother, was a magnet for scandal. *His* children wouldn't know the disgrace of living in the shadow of outrageous parents. They'd bask in the care of a beautiful, calm, respectable mother. They'd have their father's unflinching support and protection.

Never would they suffer because of their parents' behaviour. There'd be no sidelong looks of distrust as a nation waited for them to go the same way as their parents.

A wedding was necessary. But that didn't stop his desire for Cassie.

He stroked her hair. There was something about this foreign woman, something utterly missing from the paragon of female virtue he planned to wed. He needed time to explore it, savour and enjoy it.

Amir smiled and drew Cassie closer.

He'd refrain from sex this morning, but he had no intention of denying himself in the longer term. Cassie would return with him to Tarakhar as his guest, his lover, till their passion was spent.

One last affair before the business of marriage began.

Arranging the betrothal and then the wedding would take time. Time to sate himself with Cassie's unique brand of sexual allure. A mutually enjoyable interlude beckoned.

CHAPTER ELEVEN

'No, no more!' Cassie stared at the clothes spread across the embroidered coverlet and shook her head. 'Thank you, but I can't accept these.' The garments had been reverently laid out for her approval in a kaleidoscope of sumptuous fabrics, a shopaholic's dream come true.

The palace maid frowned. 'Are you sure, ma'am? There is more to come.'

'Absolutely sure.' Registering her concern, Cassie softened her words with a smile. She didn't want Amir's staff thinking she was ungrateful. 'It's all lovely, but there's more than I need. Far more.'

And more beautiful than the hard-wearing cotton and denim she'd carried in her backpack when she came to Tara-khar. Who ever heard of a volunteer teacher wearing gauzy rainbow hues spangled with semi-precious stones or edged in silver?

Though there was more to her refusal. Seeing the finery reminded her of one of the few times she'd been allowed home to her mother's chic apartment during the holidays. Her mother had been shopping with her newest lover's platinum credit card. Her bedroom had been awash with silks and lace, teetering high heels and designer handbags. Yet they'd satisfied her only for a few days, till she'd discovered some woman wearing an even newer, more expensive fashion item that she craved.

Cassie had shrunk from her mother's blatant greed even

as she'd guessed it was a sign of discontent. That her much vaunted emotion-free life hadn't made her happy. Though she'd never admit it or accept Cassie's overtures for a closer relationship.

'I only need a few things,' Cassie explained to the maid. 'This just isn't me.'

Even after bathing in a marble bath the size of a plunge pool, being anointed with attar of roses like a princess from the Arabian Nights and wearing a caftan of finest silk, Cassie knew she didn't fit in this luxurious palace.

Prisoner in that isolated mountain camp, it had been one thing to hear Amir was a king, to read in his actions and attitude that he was used to command. It was another to see evidence of his position all around her. From the servants' deep bows to the excitement of people in the street as their air-conditioned four-wheel drives passed by.

Medics had awaited them as they'd crossed the border from Bhutran. It had taken just one phone call as they rode down the mountains and out of the telecommunications black spot for a team of professionals to be on the ground.

All for her.

Amir's consideration touched a part of her that she'd learned to guard close.

Impulsively she'd turned, reached out a hand to touch him, then stopped as she'd read the carefully blank expressions on his attendants. He'd worn a mantle of aloof authority that distanced him from everyone, even her.

Especially her.

Last night's lover might never have been.

All morning he'd been reserved. A gulf had yawned between them, unbreachable and forbidding. Loss had welled in Cassie, sideswiping her with its ferocity.

Yet she'd walked into the medical tent telling herself it was for the best. Last night had been madness.

She should be grateful Amir had made it easy to put the

madness behind her. Stupidly she hadn't felt grateful. She'd felt bereft. As if something vital had been severed inside.

The thought had made her square her shoulders. Cassie didn't *do* needy.

So she'd kept her head up as she'd been escorted through the palace. Despite the dusty camel-hair cloak, she'd carried herself like a queen through elegant marble corridors and porticoes, past glimpses of richly furnished apartments and picture-perfect gardens.

Now, in this exquisite suite, she gave up pretending.

'Are you all right, ma'am?' The maid hurried over as Cassie sank into a gilded chair.

'I'm fine.' She smiled up and tried not to notice how the woman's dark eyes reminded her of Amir. They were a softer, lighter brown, not the incredible midnight-dark hue of Amir's. They didn't sizzle as his did. But—

Cassie couldn't stop thinking about him!

'I'm just tired, and probably a little too relaxed after that long soak.'

'That's good. His Highness was concerned that you rest.' She clapped her hands. Instantly a couple of women hurried in. After some brisk instructions they cleared the bed.

'If you'll permit, ma'am, I'll have a smaller selection put in your dressing room. When you're rested you can choose which you'd like to keep.'

'Thank you.' Cassie smiled gratefully. It was stupid even to think it, but for a moment, looking at the display of beautiful clothes laid out, the suspicion had crossed her mind that Amir was paying for her services last night. A preposterous idea, but unsettling.

'Is there anything else I can get you?'

'No, thanks.' There was a myriad of things Cassie should be doing—organising a passport to replace the one she'd lost, accessing her bank account and letting the volunteer programme people know where she was. Yet it seemed too much effort. 'I think I'll rest now.'

Moments later Cassie was alone. She was safe and cared for. It was absurd to feel a sense of loss. Yet it pooled within her, grim and undeniable.

For the man who'd been her lover such a short time.

A prickle of sensation spread under her skin. Amir had been fierce yet gentle, demanding yet considerate. They'd shared things she'd never dreamed of.

Flattening her lips as they began to curve into a besotted smile, Cassie shot to her feet.

Probably most women felt this...*yearning* for their first lover. It *had* only been last night. She'd barely had time to assimilate what had happened before she was chivvied out of the tent for their perilous descent down the mountains.

She should be thankful there'd been no time for awkwardness. Much easier to act as if nothing had happened, as Amir did.

Cassie folded her arms and paced to the window.

She'd initiated their lovemaking. Sex was what she'd wanted. An antidote to the crawling tension that had filled her for a week, and to the stirrings of desire she'd felt for the first time. A way to overcome the murky fear that had surfaced at the idea of being intimate with a man.

So why was she battling distress because Amir kept his distance? Why did she long for a tender look?

She should be pleased he realised what they'd shared was over. That he didn't press for more.

The idea of Amir wanting more made her breath hitch. Her hand shot out to the window frame for support. For a split second she let herself imagine her and Amir together as a couple, not for a night but for much more.

'No!' Cassie spun on her foot and headed into the garden. She was strong and independent. She'd weave no foolish dreams about any man.

Dusk had fallen when Amir went in search of her. His spurt of anxiety on discovering her rooms empty disturbed him. The bottom had dropped from his stomach till he'd seen the open door and realised she'd gone into the garden.

Now, watching her sleep, he assured himself it was normal to feel relief that she was OK. She was his guest, his responsibility.

His lover.

His gaze trailed over her sinuous curves as she sprawled on the day bed in a secluded garden pavilion. The air was heavy with the scent of roses and she lay like an innocent seductress, one hand beneath her cheek, the other flung wide so he had an unimpaired view of her perfect breasts rising and falling beneath fine silk.

He closed the door and paced close.

On his return he'd been sucked into the business of ruling. Agreements, agendas and annotations. He'd met officials and dealt with a few crises.

Yet his mind had been fixed on her. It had taken all his effort not to shove aside his work and go to her. He told himself it was the novelty of their relationship. Lust, in the early stages, was incredibly distracting.

Yet how long since he'd felt one-fifth of this fascination for a woman? His interest in affairs had waned as boredom with his partners' over-eagerness took over.

In his early thirties and he'd grown jaded with the predictable!

In some ways he *was* like his father. But whereas his father had sought distraction in vice and mindless pleasure, Amir could control temptation.

Amir sank onto the bed, one arm braced over Cassie's hip. He lifted his hand and delicately circled one nipple with the tip of his finger. It peaked and he recalled her responsiveness last night when he'd taken that taut bud in his mouth.

Smiling, he touched his lips to that sensitive peak.

She stirred. Drowsily her eyes opened, dark violet and velvety with pleasure.

* * *

Amir was here. The laxness in her muscles, the heat in her blood convinced her it was no dream, even as her eyes opened and she found him, black eyes riveted on hers.

'Amir!' So right did it seem, it took a moment to shake the cobwebs of sleep away. When she did, Cassie shot a horrified look towards the door. 'What are you doing? Anyone might come in!'

She surged up, pushing him away, swinging her legs over the edge of the divan and rising on unsteady legs.

'No one will intrude, *habibti*, not without permission. These grounds are for my exclusive use and yours.'

Something about the deep, proprietorial tone made her brow pucker. He hadn't been so interested in her this morning when she'd sought his reassurance.

'As for what I'm doing.' His mouth lifted in a rare smile and, despite her misgivings, Cassie felt its impact deep inside. 'I was caressing my lover.'

My lover. In that resonant drawl the words stirred magic in her soul.

Till she reminded herself he'd withdrawn from her all day. He'd been aloof, not sparing her a private word, and acting as if last night hadn't happened. Despite her determination to treat it as a one-night stand, his behaviour hurt. It smacked of off-hand dismissal.

It reminded her of the cool attitude of her mother's lovers. Each had expected his mistress to be available on tap, but had never bothered to think about her needs.

Cassie moved away.

'I'm not your lover.'

Amir stood and Cassie's gaze clung to his rangy form, clad this time in tailored trousers and shirt. He looked mouth-wateringly gorgeous with his sleeves rolled to reveal the corded muscle of his forearms. His collar was undone, drawing her eyes to the V of golden skin against the pure white cotton.

'Are you not?' Sleek brows pinched in disapproval as he stalked closer.

If she hadn't experienced Amir's tenderness she'd have retreated in the face of what looked like searing anger. As it was, trepidation shivered through her.

Her chin shot up. 'We had one night together. That's all.' She told herself that was all she wanted. One night out of time to experience such heady delights. Any more would be too dangerous. Too addictive.

He paced closer, stopped when his breath hazed her cheek and her skin contracted in response. Her nipples stood proud and pouting, as if inviting his touch, and between her thighs moist heat bloomed.

Her cheeks flamed as she registered how her body prepared itself for his possession. As if he only had to touch her and she'd give herself to him!

'Why not share more than a single night?' The words, pure temptation, swirled soft as thought on the air.

Because Amir scrambled her brains. He uncorked longings she'd barely known she harboured.

Because she was scared if she didn't make the break now it would be impossible to drag herself away.

Because she'd had a taste of what it was like to be dismissed by him. It made her feel…vulnerable.

'You didn't seem so interested in me this morning!' She kept her voice cool, but inside shreds of hurt whirled and accumulated, weighing her heart. 'There was no private discussion. Not so much as a look. For all I knew I'd never see you again!'

That had frightened her far too much.

'Cassandra.' His voice was seductively low. 'I'm sorry.' He lifted his hand towards her cheek but checked himself, his fingers mere centimetres from her face.

Yet she *felt* him as if he'd touched her!

'I sought to protect you from gossip and discomfort. Bad enough that my staff know you were given to me as a sex slave.' His look was grim. 'I tried to counter that by ensuring Faruq knew how things were between us until last night. He would have made that known to rest of my staff. My aim today was to reinforce that. To treat you with respect so others would too.'

'Really?' The notion hadn't entered her head. All she'd known was lacerating pain and a sense of shame she couldn't quite suppress when he'd seemed to spurn her. The possibility he'd attempted to protect her took a lot of assimilating.

Yet hadn't he cared for her? Hadn't he kept his distance as much as he could till last night?

'The people of Tarakhar are good people, but they are easily influenced in matters of reputation. Believe me; I know what I'm talking about.'

The steel in his words grabbed her attention and threatened to divert her.

'Besides, what's between us is private.'

The gleam in his eyes was nearly irresistible and Cassie's heart flipped over.

'You could have said something. Given some indication.'

Slowly he nodded, his gaze never wavering. 'Would it surprise you to know I was scared of what would happen if I did? The compulsion to touch you, kiss you and hold you close has driven me insane all day.'

Fingers of heat spread through Cassie as she heard truth ring in his words.

Logic told her to break this relationship, such as it was, before she got in too deep. Yet her overwhelming feelings were relief and excitement. He wanted more, as she did. She wasn't alone in experiencing this overwhelming need.

'I can't imagine you scared.'

His lips twisted wryly. 'A man doesn't like to lose control. Especially a man like me. And you, *habibti*, are too dangerous a test of my restraint.'

Cassie followed his look to where his hand hovered close to her face. It was unsteady.

Like her limbs that trembled from his nearness.

In that moment, like the single powerful stroke that sliced the Gordian knot, Cassie felt tension and doubt disintegrate in a violent rush of relief.

This was mutual. Amir wanted her as she did him. More, he was honest about it, treating her as an equal. He'd been genuinely considerate in attempting to prevent gossip.

'I want you, Cassie.' The words devastated thought. 'Do you still want me?'

Silently she nodded.

'Then why not share this passion a little longer?'

His eyes flared, reminding her of the conflagration that had consumed them last night. A delicious shudder racked her body.

She wanted to. How she wanted to.

Yet was it wise?

Suddenly it struck Cassie that, far from being strong all these years, she'd lived in fear. She'd let the past dictate her life, scared of repeating her mother's mistakes or laying herself open to manipulation. Had she used that as an excuse to hide from her own sexuality?

The disturbing notion wouldn't shift.

What Amir offered wasn't manipulation. It was mutual pleasure and respect.

How could that be bad?

'I'm here in Tarakhar for a reason. I can't just forget that.' It was a last-ditch attempt to resist the irresistible.

Amir's eyes narrowed as if displeased. Then he shrugged. 'I'm sure that can be accommodated. After all, you'll need time to sort out your travel documents and so on. There's no rush to leave, and you're welcome to enjoy my hospitality for as long as you desire.'

Desire. The word shivered through her very bones.

The evening air hung still. Even the end-of-day chatter of the birds faded as Cassie tried to weigh this sensibly. But it wasn't logic that dictated her response. It was something far more visceral.

'I'd like to stay.' She paused and swiped her tongue around suddenly dry lips.

Relief was the warmth of his hand cradling her jaw, his thumb brushing her cheek. It was the sight of his rare smile and the answering sunburst of sensation within her.

Amir stepped in, his body hard against her, his head swooping in a kiss that claimed her breath and her mind.

It felt like hours later that Cassie lay, sated and dreamy, within the circle of Amir's embrace. The cushions from the day bed had fallen to the floor and their clothes were strewn there too. But here in her lover's arms she felt content, warm and happy.

Despite the lingering niggle that she'd jumped into a situation without due thought, she sensed she'd made the right decision. All her life she'd let instinct guide her, and she prayed it wouldn't lead her astray now.

Something tickled at her waist and she stirred. It took a moment to realise it was Amir, stroking her skin. Lazily she smiled. He couldn't seem to get enough of touching her and she loved it.

She opened her eyes. In the gloom of early evening she could make out the avid glitter in his gaze as he traced the line of the chain still encircling her.

'You promised to help me get rid of that when we got back to civilisation.'

'Did I?'

Concentration pleated his brow as he slipped his hand under the links, palm flat to her skin.

It was impossible after their tumultuous lovemaking that Cassie should feel arousal stir, yet she did. The intensity of his regard and the languid sensuality of his touch awoke an instantaneous response.

'Yes. As soon as we got here, you said.'

Amir breathed deep and met her eyes.

'As you wish.' He didn't sound enthusiastic.

Puzzled, Cassie tilted her head. Then understanding struck. 'You *like* it! You enjoy seeing it there!'

At her accusing tone he shrugged. 'It accentuates your waist and your curves.' He paused. 'It's very sexy.'

She shook her head. 'It's a slave chain! It's a symbol that I'm not my own woman. That I—'

'That you're mine.' At her shocked stare he smiled gently and lifted his hand to skim his knuckles across her cheek. 'Don't worry, Cassie. I understand how you feel. I know it's untenable.' His eyes darkened. 'But I'm man enough to respond to it even though it's not politically correct. I love the idea that, for now, you're mine.' His voice vibrated with a possessiveness that echoed to her core. 'Not by force but by choice.'

Shocked, Cassie stared up, reading the truth in his lazily lidded eyes.

'You wouldn't feel that way if I suggested roping you to my bed so you couldn't get away.'

Heat glazed his eyes as he stared at her mouth, then at her breasts. His lips lifted in a smile of devastating sensuality.

When he looked up Cassie's pulse hammered out of control. Her skin tingled as if he'd trailed his fingers over every erogenous zone in her body.

'I don't know about that.' Amir leaned close and his words were hot on her sensitive flesh. 'I've never been into bondage. Yet I have a feeling I might enjoy it. With you.'

Cassie swallowed hard at the image he conjured. That oh-so-lazily sexy smile and his deep, deep voice tugged at places inside she'd barely been aware of.

Far from being horrified or outraged, she knew it was excitement that thrilled through her.

The idea of being *possessed*, of being claimed so blatantly by a man, should be anathema to her. In the camp the idea had made her skin crawl.

Yet now with Amir it was different—and not solely because

he spoke of her choosing to be his. Perversely she discovered a sense of power in the fact he wanted her so much. To her shock, the idea of having him at her mercy sexually held a forbidden allure she'd never thought possible.

Cassie's eyes widened. In agreeing to be Amir's lover she'd stepped from safety into the dark unknown.

She couldn't pull back. The allure was too strong. Her need was too intense. *She wanted everything he offered.*

'I see you understand,' he purred against her mouth, then swiped the tip of his tongue between her parted lips in a sensual promise of pleasure to come.

Too soon he pulled away.

'Dinner,' he said huskily. 'Our meal has no doubt been waiting for some time and you need your strength.' The twinkle in his eyes warmed her. 'Then I'll find something to cut those links.'

CHAPTER TWELVE

'AMIR?'

'Hmm?' Long fingers tangled with hers even as Amir focused on the chessboard. As ever, he threatened to distract her with the lightest touch, reminding her of the bliss they'd shared.

In the late-night stillness they might have been the only residents of the sprawling palace.

Cassie loved this time. Precious hours together when Amir finished his work and she came alive to his lovemaking. Sex with Amir had gone from spectacular to spellbinding as under his tutelage, she'd learned to listen to the needs of her body, and his, enjoying both to the full.

Yet, more than sex, Cassie enjoyed these times when, not driven by desire, they lounged, relaxed and companionable.

It was something she'd never before experienced—sharing.

They played chess or talked of anything from politics to town planning, about the theatre or music. They swam by moonlight in Amir's private pool lined with exquisite handmade mosaic tiles. Once Amir had driven her out to a lookout from where she'd seen the lights of the capital spread below her, like a glittering reflection of the starry sky above. On the way back she'd been enchanted by glimpses of the colourful night markets in full swing and vowed to revisit during the day.

Amir lifted her hand and pressed a kiss to it, sending her

thoughts spinning just as he moved his queen across the board. 'Check.'

Cassie laughed, albeit breathlessly. 'You're trying to distract me so you'll win.'

His eyebrows rose in mock surprise, belied by the glitter in his eyes. 'Will it work?'

She struggled against the tide of tenderness that rose when he teased her. 'Of course not.' She straightened and concentrated on the board, pulling her hand free.

'I spoke to the volunteer agency today. I told them I'm not ready to go to that school just yet.'

'Good.' Amir moved to sit beside her. His arm slipped around her waist.

Amir had been adamant she wasn't ready to leave the city and she'd agreed. Not because of lingering trauma, but because she didn't want to leave him.

'But there's work here in the city. Tomorrow I'll begin with a small English-language class.'

'Tomorrow? Impossible!'

Cassie turned and looked up at him. His aristocratically honed features looked tight.

'Why?'

He frowned. 'You've had a traumatic experience.'

Cassie smiled and lifted her hand to his face, stroking the deep groove that had formed at the corner of his mouth. It always struck her as incredibly sexy.

'You've helped me get over it.' Still he didn't smile. 'I'm *fine*, Amir. You know that.'

'You can't *want* to go there.'

She tilted her head as she surveyed him. 'Of course I want to go. What have I got to do here?'

'Am I not enough for you?'

Instantly Cassie stiffened. The smile bled from her face as she saw he was serious. With an effort she stifled her rising temper.

'I see you at night, Amir. That's all. During the day I've

nothing to do. I've got no occupation. I've got no companions. Even though your staff are friendly that's not the same.' She paused and drew a deep breath, focused on keeping her tone reasonable.

It didn't help that an insidious voice inside whispered that he wanted her at his beck and call, reminding her that her mother had lived solely to service a man's desires. This was different. *Wasn't it?*

'I don't see you giving up your work to spend all your time with me.'

'Of course not.' Some of the tension in his face eased, yet he didn't look happy.

'Of course not,' Cassie echoed. 'I wouldn't expect it.'

Her soft fingers stilled against his cheek and Amir covered them with his, revelling in the feel of her here, where he wanted her.

Where he needed her.

Where had that come from?

Amir ibn Masud Al Jaber didn't need anyone. He never had.

Yet the denial didn't ring true. At this moment he needed the reassurance of Cassie's touch, her warmth, as he'd never remembered needing anyone.

The realisation crashed through him.

He drew a breath, centring himself after the shock. Not at her statement that she wanted to work, but at his intense visceral reaction. What he'd felt in that moment was a possessiveness so crude, so primitive, it made a mockery of his claim to be a modern civilised man.

'This is important to you?'

Amir felt her tension ease as the militant light in her eyes faded. How often had he let himself fall headlong into those pansy-dark depths, transfixed by Cassie's unique passion? A passion for life as well as for pleasure.

'Of course it's important. That's why I came to Tarakhar. I want to do something useful. I love acting but right now it doesn't seem enough. I want something more tangible, at least for a while.'

Fleetingly Amir thought of the many women he'd known only too eager to live off his generosity in idle luxury.

'You want to leave your mark?'

She shrugged. 'You could put it like that. It just seems a shame not to contribute more. I like the idea of being part of something bigger than myself.'

Amir remembered what she'd said about her childhood, not being wanted by either parent. Cassie talked blithely of friends, and with her outgoing personality he was sure there were plenty, but she'd never spoken of anyone especially close. Was her determination to work in a foreign language and literacy programme spurred by her desire to belong? To be needed?

He pursed his lips. Why was he delving so deep, puzzling out every nuance?

Because Cassie was important to him.

A frisson of premonition feathered through him. Or was that warning?

These days he thought of Cassie more and more, even when he should be concentrating on the mass of royal work. His thoughts lingered not only on sex, but on how he enjoyed her company, the way she made him feel.

He stiffened, uneasy with the direction of his thoughts.

Having her occupied elsewhere would be good for them both. He didn't want her getting notions about a permanent place in his life.

What they had was perfect while it lasted. Mutual pleasure with no strings attached. He shoved to one side the lurking suspicion that soon he might want more. Such an eventuality would not occur.

'What's important to you, Amir?'

Startled, he focused on Cassie's upturned face. She looked so earnest.

'No one's ever asked me that before.'

In truth, he'd rarely considered it himself—except as a child, when he'd craved...love, he supposed. Then as an adolescent all he'd wanted was to prove himself and *belong*. Carve a place for himself in this new world of Tarakhar where, despite the frowns and misgivings over the son of a scoundrel, he'd discovered stability and honour and finally a home.

It struck him that perhaps he and Cassie had been driven by similar demons.

Though of course he'd vanquished his. As sheikh of a populous and prosperous country he had other concerns than the shadows of his past.

Cassie watched Amir's eyes flicker as if processing memories. What was he thinking?

'Let me guess what's important to you.' She leaned across and moved one of the beautifully carved antique pieces on the chessboard. 'Winning at chess.'

'Winning at everything.' A smile softened his words but they had the ring of truth.

'Really?'

He nodded. 'If anything's worth doing, it's worth doing well.'

Cassie's breath snagged as her brain diverted to what they'd been doing half an hour ago. She remembered his absolute concentration on giving her pleasure, the way he'd drawn out each caress till she was almost screaming with the pleasure-pain of arousal and need.

If something was worth doing...

No wonder he was such an exquisitely generous lover.

'What else?' Her voice was husky and she cleared her throat.

Amir moved a piece to corner her king. 'My people. My country.'

'But it wasn't always that way? Didn't you say you rebelled at one time?'

He shrugged. 'When I was young and impatient I had other

interests. At first I tried to be all they expected and more. I had to work twice as hard as anyone else. To be accepted I had to be not only competent but perfect at every task. And still everyone waited for me to run riot, just like my notorious parents.'

Cassie knew what it was like to be the child of notorious parents. School had often been hellish because someone had seen Cassie's mum at the races or the theatre on the arm of her latest paramour. Everyone knew she'd been bought and paid for, just like a new watch or a car.

'Finally I'd had enough. I decided I might as well fulfil everyone's expectations.' Amir's voice dropped to a pitch that made something quiver inside.

'What did you do?'

'I devoted myself to pleasure and nothing else. I went on a binge of parties, gambling and overindulgence of colossal proportions. I doubt I was sober one day in four.'

'And?'

'And what?'

'What changed?'

Amir's eyebrows rose and he pulled her hand towards him, bending to draw his tongue along her palm till she trembled and edged closer.

'Persistent, aren't you?'

'I want to know.' It surprised her exactly how much she wanted to know about Amir.

He shrugged, and she hated the hard edge of cynicism in his voice when he spoke again. 'At first it was exciting, satisfying, even. No rules, no regimen. Just pleasure.' His lips thinned in a tight smile. 'Then I woke one morning with a woman I couldn't remember. Her body was a testament to surgical enhancement in too many places to count. She had a plastic smile, eyes that flashed dollar signs, and a laugh like an asthmatic mule, guaranteed to tip a man into insanity after twenty-four hours.'

Cassie curved her mouth in a perfunctory smile at his

humour, but inside sadness carved a hollow. What a waste of a man like Amir.

'I had no idea whose apartment I was in, much less which country. I couldn't remember the previous week, but I had no trouble realising I was utterly, irredeemably bored.' He shook his head abruptly. 'I looked in the mirror that morning and for the first time ever saw my father's face looking back at me.'

'You didn't like your father?' She could relate to that.

Amir threaded his fingers though hers and looked down at their joined hands as if they held some great truth.

'You have to know someone to dislike them, don't you?'

When she didn't speak he shrugged again, and his breath escaped in a low rush.

'I never knew my parents. They were strangers to me. I was cared for most of the time by the staff at whatever resort they were staying at.'

'And the rest of the time?'

Amir lifted his gaze and Cassie was shocked by the fierce blankness she read there.

'The rest of the time I wasn't cared for.'

She flinched with shock and he turned his attention back to her hand, trailing his index finger over each of hers in a deliberately erotic caress, as if to distract her from his words. It didn't work, though deep inside the flicker of awareness that was ever-present near Amir burst into pulsing life.

'One of my earliest memories is waking to find my room being made up by an unfamiliar maid who didn't speak any language I knew. My parents had been invited to a party weekend in the Alps and had left instantly. Unfortunately they'd forgotten, till they got a call on arrival in Switzerland, that they'd left me behind in Rio de Janeiro.'

'Oh, Amir!' She curved her hand into his, cupped her other hand around them as if she could somehow erase the pain of such neglect. She'd never felt wanted, and had been told time and again she'd ruined her mother's life, but her mother had never forgotten she existed! How could his parents have cared so little? 'How old were you?'

'I don't know. Three? Maybe four?'

Cassie's heart thundered with outrage and distress at what such a childhood must have been like.

'It's all right, Cassie.' With his free hand he brushed his knuckles over her cheek. 'I survived. And when they died I came here to my uncle.'

The uncle who'd spent his days watching his nephew like a hawk, waiting for the day the telltale weakness of his parents would reveal itself.

What sort of life was that for a child? The fire burning in her belly had nothing to do with arousal, but with a fierce need to protect the boy Amir had been.

'After my taste of reckless living I ended up back here,' Amir continued. 'Not because I was ordered to but because I knew I'd do anything rather than turn into my father. Because this was what I wanted—this place, these people. I needed purpose and stability. I turned my life around and made a place for myself. I faced down the doubters and proved myself so well that when my uncle died the Council of Elders turned to me rather than my older cousin to lead the country. This is my destiny.'

His hand dropped from her cheek and he withdrew his other hand from her grasp.

She missed his touch so much it frightened her.

'My sons will grow up with a father to be proud of. A respectable mother, not a notorious one. There'll be no taint of scandal marring their lives. They'll be cared for and cherished, accepted by everyone.'

His words rang with a certainty she almost envied.

For a moment, before she realised where her thoughts had strayed, Cassie found herself wishing he'd look at *her* as he spoke of his wife and future family. How wonderful it would be if…

No! Such thoughts were dangerous.

Amir knew exactly what he wanted. He'd planned it all out. Whereas Cassie knew what she *didn't* want. A life without respect or choice. A life dependent on the whims of a man who didn't love her.

Yet surely now she was taking steps towards a more positive focus? With Amir's help she'd banished the dark demons of fear. She enjoyed to the full every moment with this remarkable man. A man so strong and honourable he banished her preconceived biases. A man so honest and forthright she could share anything. A man so tender he opened new worlds of delight.

Plus she felt so good about this new work she was planning. If she could make a difference in someone's life maybe that would give her the purpose she'd lacked.

What more could she possibly want?

'There's one more thing, Highness.'

Amir heard the hesitation in Faruq's voice and looked up sharply. His aide was anything but comfortable.

'Everything's in place in Bhutran, isn't it?' It had been weeks since they'd left the mountains and Amir grew impatient to conclude his unfinished business with Mustafa. The memory of what had been done to Cassie made him long for retribution.

'Yes. The situation will be dealt with in the next few days.'

'The situation' being Mustafa.

Despite the negotiations, and Mustafa's promises, the old renegade showed his true colours with continued incursions into Tarakhar, breaking every promise.

If necessary Amir would put an end to that with an incursion of his own that would topple Mustafa from his comfortable mountain perch.

But it seemed that wouldn't be necessary. Changes in Bhutran meant that a newly energised central government, eager to maintain peace with its neighbours, was moving against Mustafa and others like him.

Amir had conveniently supplied information on the size and location of his camp, and offered back-up should it be necessary.

Soon there would be peace on the border and Mustafa would be a spent force. Satisfaction filled Amir.

'Good.' He nodded and stood, stretching, behind his desk. It had been a long day and he'd promised himself the pleasure of an early visit to Cassie. Strange how her allure grew with each passing day instead of diminishing.

'It's about Ms Denison, Sire.'

Amir's head whipped round. Cassie wasn't a subject he shared with anyone. 'What about her?'

Faruq stood straighter, as if preparing to defend himself.

'I wondered how long she would remain in residence.'

Amir's eyebrows shot up. 'As long as I wish her to remain.'

'Of course. It's just that…'

'Yes?'

'The betrothal negotiations are nearing completion.' Faruq spread his hands in a stiff gesture of appeal. 'Ms Denison's continued presence in the palace has become a matter of speculation.'

Amir strode from behind the desk to the far side of the room, his hands clenched in tight fists behind him.

'Ms Denison is my guest. She is recuperating from a violent assault.'

'Of course, Highness.' Yet the tone of Faruq's agreement wasn't convincing.

'What are they saying?'

Faruq shrugged. 'There is speculation that you and she…'

Naturally there was speculation. How could he have thought otherwise? A beautiful woman living unchaperoned in his palace, albeit on the other side of the building from his own suite.

He'd never invited a woman to stay in his home. He'd kept his liaisons discreetly away from the palace. He'd considered installing Cassie in a convenient apartment but that wouldn't do. Amir wanted her *here*.

Their affair had barely begun. He had no intention of denying himself. Cassie was a feast for the intellect as well as the body, with her active mind and her interest in everything. One minute she was mimicking the self-conscious pomp of his chamberlain strutting the corridors, and the next she was asking penetrating questions about the state of education in Tarakhar. Or sharing her body with an almost innocent generosity and delight that sometimes made him wonder if she could be nearly as experienced as her sassy attitude suggested.

'I do not concern myself with idle gossip.' Short of providing Cassie with a personal chaperon, which would be a farce as well as an inconvenience, there was little he could do to prevent talk. 'Ms Denison is a private guest, not a public figure.'

'Of course, Sire.' Faruq nodded but didn't move away. He drew a deep breath and Amir sensed his reluctance to continue.

'What is it, Faruq?' Impatience rose, but the man had a job to do. Barking at him wouldn't stop him. That was why Amir liked him, he took his work seriously. 'You'd better tell me.'

'I fear it's not quite that simple. While Ms Denison *is* your private guest, she's hardly invisible. With her colouring she draws attention wherever she goes in the old city. Far from being discreet, she's becoming something of a local celebrity.'

'Indeed?' This was the first Amir had heard of it.

'Yes. Instead of holding classes on the premises provided, she takes her pupils out. They hold impromptu lessons in the market or the park, at the library and in the new art gallery. Even at the railway station.'

Amir's lips twitched at the image of Cassie and her small group of women practising their English on a railway platform. Why didn't it surprise him? It was just like Cassie to ditch the stuffy classroom for places where language could be demonstrated in action.

'I hardly see this as a problem.'

Faruq spread his hands. 'By all accounts the students are enthusiastic and the classes are popular. But when forty people gather in a transport hub or at a public building, they attract a lot of attention. Ms Denison and her students are becoming well-known.'

'Forty people? I was told it was a small language class for women who hadn't completed school. Half a dozen participants.'

Faruq nodded. 'It's growing daily. There's talk of extra classes, with more teachers to spread the load.' He paused. 'It's a great initiative, Sire, but not designed to help her keep a low profile. In fact…'

'Well?' Amir frowned. He couldn't begrudge Cassie her success with the classes. She'd described them enthusiastically but in general terms, saying the students were coming on well and mentioning some of the language issues they faced. He'd had no idea how successful they were. Her dedication to the project was clear, and the benefits to his people were equally apparent.

'The gossip has spread as far as your intended's father.' Faruq shot him a hurried glance, then looked down at his hands. 'He has expressed a query, couched in the most delicate of terms, about the…*longevity* of the situation.'

'Has he indeed?'

Anger roiled in Amir's belly that the man had the temerity to query his Sheikh's intentions. He sold his daughter in marriage to the highest bidder. The fact that it was Amir who'd snared the prize only inflated the man's ego.

'Should anyone ask, Ms Denison is making an indefinite stay. You can take it from me this has no relevance to my marriage arrangements. It's purely a private matter.'

CHAPTER THIRTEEN

'I HEAR your classes are a raging success.'

Cassie spun round as Amir's deep voice broke her concentration. It was late afternoon and she was making notes for tomorrow's class.

'Amir! What are you doing here so early?' Her voice was breathless, as if his sudden appearance was the most important thing that had happened in her day.

If only that weren't true!

It shocked her the way she came alive in his presence, as if the rest of the day was sepia-toned and only burst into Technicolor when he was here. Even the satisfaction she got from her classes, from interacting with the other women and learning a little about this fascinating city, paled into insignificance against the thrill of being with Amir.

Every evening it grew harder to let him walk away. She wanted to hold him so he stayed the night. Wake in his arms to the sound of his low voice rumbling through her and feel the harsh caress of his stubble on her skin.

She'd never have thought it possible but she missed the tent they'd shared. The intimacy of waking with him.

The palace was so huge and she'd got lost more than once trying to find her way to Amir, only to meet his stuffy chamberlain who'd inform her with exquisite politeness that His Highness could not be disturbed.

'I'm visiting you.' As ever, something melted inside her at the rich caress of Amir's voice. 'If you'll permit.'

Cassie soaked up the sight of him, tall and magnificent even in a casual white shirt and worn jeans that emphasised his lean masculine strength.

He stole her breath every time! Her heart pounded a faster beat.

'Of course.' She tried to sound casual but failed. Her breath hitched when he strode across the room, his eyes alight like a marauding bandit spying booty. An instant later he plucked Cassie from her seat, roped his arms around her and dragged her close.

His kiss was an explosive mix of demand and hunger with a hint of seduction that made her weak at the knees.

Cassie grabbed his shoulders and hung on as her body softened into his, returning his kiss with a fervour that even after all these weeks hadn't abated one bit.

She *loved* his kisses.

She loved the way he made her feel when he held her close. She loved his strength and tenderness. His honour and his concern for her. The way he teased straight-faced so it took her a moment to read the humour in his gleaming eyes. She loved…

Cassie's brain fused as a blast of white-hot power surged through her. A blast of revelation.

Gasping, she pulled her mouth from his and looked up into those long-lashed eyes that saw so deeply.

Did they see what she was thinking now?

No! Panic buzzed through her and she stepped back, only to be stopped by Amir's arms, linked hard around her body. Her pulse raced and hectic colour seared her cheeks.

'Cassie? Are you OK?'

Quickly she nodded, her tongue glued to the roof of her mouth by shock.

Desperately she tried to convince herself she was mistaken. The thought that had frozen her brain was so earth-shattering it couldn't be true.

Could it?

Amir raised one hand and stroked his thumb over her bottom lip. Tiny shards of arousal zigzagged through her.

A physical response, she assured herself. They were lovers and sexual pleasure was what kept them together.

But not all.

There it was again, that unsettling idea zipping through her brain and sending her into turmoil.

The idea that she...*loved* Amir!

'Cassandra?'

Her heart flip-flopped at the way he said her name in full. It never failed to affect her. Would it still affect her in six months? In six years? In sixty?

Stupid to form the question. There was no doubt, Cassie realised as a strange serenity settled upon her. Of course it would. And she would still care for *him*.

She'd fallen for Amir. Not for the pleasure they shared but for the man himself.

Part of her brain tried to shout a warning, but it was overwhelmed by a rush of endorphins, a wave of warm delight that filled her at the thought.

Amir.

The man she loved.

'You look different.'

'I do?' She smiled up into his concerned expression and almost blurted her revelation. But even the euphoria of self-realisation couldn't blot out the knowledge that this complicated everything.

What, exactly, did Amir feel for her?

'Hmm, could it be the stylish new way I've done my hair?' She tried to distract him with a smile, pretending to primp as if professionally coiffed instead of wearing the lop-sided ponytail she'd quickly created as she'd pulled her hair out of her eyes to read.

'Undoubtedly, *habibti*.' He kissed her hand and, as ever, her knees weakened. 'You are the loveliest teacher in the whole of the capital.'

'Flatterer!' Yet her heart sang at the gleam in his eyes.

'Never.' He lifted her hand and pressed his lips to the fluttering pulse at her wrist. Cassie felt the kernel of warmth inside glow brighter and spread. Oh, she had it bad.

'I'd like to talk with you about your classes, but first, are you free for an excursion? There's something I want to show you.'

An outing with Amir? 'I'd love to. Where are we going?'

'It's tremendous,' Cassie declared. 'You must be very pleased.' In all honesty it was the thrill of being out with Amir, sharing something of his world, that excited her most, but this was spectacular.

Below this knoll wound a canal, its curve mimicking the sinuous course of a river. Mature trees had been planted in groves that would provide shade, and more were waiting to be set in place by earth-moving equipment.

Now, bathed in dusk's indigo shadows, it was easy to imagine the broad corridor of parkland as it would be when complete.

'There's the site of the new hospital.' Cassie followed Amir's gesture to the right, where the building site was almost encircled by what would one day be public parkland. 'Over there is the medical research facility completed last year, and there—' he pointed to an area on the other side of the water '—the route of the new light railway that will give access to the medical precinct and pleasure gardens.'

Cassie surveyed the kiosks dotting the parkland, the massive adventure playground, swimming centre and the intriguing foundations of a maze.

'It will be a perfect place for families.' She could imagine coming here in the cool of morning or late afternoon. Listening to children's laughter and excited shouts as they explored. One day she'd love to picnic here, watching her children play.

It took a moment to absorb where her thoughts had strayed. To realise it was Amir she imagined sharing the picnic blanket with her. That the toddlers in her mind's eye had laughing dark eyes and golden-toned skin like the man beside her.

Cassie's heart lurched. Did Amir want children? Or marriage? This project, funded from his personal coffers, seemed to indicate an interest not only in modern infrastructure but in providing amenities for families.

Perhaps one day—

'I'm glad you approve, Cassie.' His hand on hers cut across her thoughts and she struggled to compose herself. 'It's been one of my pet projects.'

When she turned it was to see him pull a small pouch from his pocket.

'I have something for you, *habibti*.'

He extended his hand. On his palm lay a large teardrop stone of deep blue-violet that seemed to glow inside. Cassie's breath escaped in a hiss and her hand crept to her throat.

'You like it?'

Silently she nodded, stunned by its beauty. The stone was faceted to catch the light, and even in the dimming afternoon it sparkled with a thousand stars.

She couldn't shake the conviction this was some priceless gem he'd spied in the palace treasure house or, given the streamlined modern chain, a high-class jeweller's showroom. Yet surely not even a royal sheikh would give a real gem of that size on a whim?

Nevertheless, a sour taste tainted her mouth as she remembered the expensive diamond brooch of which her mother had been so proud. Given not with love but as part of her purchase price. Pricey gifts had been part of her arrangement with each new protector.

Cassie shivered. Instantly Amir's hand gripped her shoulder. 'Cassie?'

'It's not…?' She swiped her tongue over dry lips, needing to know but not wanting to chance the possibility she was right. 'It looks very expensive, Amir. I don't feel comfortable accepting it.'

Strong fingers tilted her chin till she was looking up into eyes that glittered brighter than the dazzling stone.

'Your scruples do you credit.' He smiled and the sombre lines around his mouth vanished. 'But you're mistaken if you think this some family heirloom. It's just a pretty stone, a trinket that caught my eye.'

'It's kind of you, Amir, but I can't take it.'

'It's not kind at all.' Something flashed in his eyes. 'I saw it and it reminded me of you: its colour, its vibrancy.' His words, like caresses, curled around her eager heart. It grew harder every moment to resist.

'You accept nothing from me but the roof over your head and the meals provided by my kitchens. You spurn every gift I try to give, even something as trifling as a chess set.'

Amir's voice echoed with disappointment and what she could almost convince herself was hurt.

'Even the clothes to replace the wardrobe you lost were too much to accept without limitations.' His hand slashed impatiently. 'Most of it you sent back.'

Cassie stared, stunned by the intensity of his feelings. Had she been churlish with her continual refusals? 'I didn't mean to offend you.'

Amir nodded, the militant spark fading as his expression softened. 'No offence taken.' He stroked her cheek with his knuckles. 'Wear it for me? It would make me happy.'

'It's utterly gorgeous.' She summoned a bright smile for Amir, firmly banishing the shades of the past and focusing on the man she loved.

Amir wasn't buying her with expensive jewellery, as her mother had been bought. He'd found a trinket of costume jewellery that to her untutored eyes looked stunningly expensive. But what did she know of gems? He'd thought to give her pleasure. *That* was what counted.

Happiness surged anew as she looked into his face. This time her smile was completely genuine.

His mouth brushed hers and she leaned in close, but too

soon he pulled away, mischief lurking in his eyes. 'Let me put this on you.'

Amir had chosen a long chain, so the stone nestled low between her breasts, which entailed undoing buttons on her silk shirt so the necklace could be appreciated properly.

Fortunately they were completely alone. There was no one to see as Amir bent to feather kisses across the top of her breasts, or as she clung needily to his shoulders.

Amir pressed another kiss to Cassie's sweet skin, then centred the pendant carefully between her breasts, enjoying the perfection of it against her gleaming satin flesh.

He wanted her to wear the gem always. Not because it was worth a fortune, but because he liked the idea she wore *his* gift so intimately.

'You'll wear this for me?' The words came out husky and he swallowed an unfamiliar constriction in his throat.

'If you like.'

'I like.'

'I like too. It's beautiful. Thank you.' Her smile warmed his soul as she lifted her hand to stroke his cheek.

Desire stirred. He clamped her hand in his and pressed a kiss to her palm, surprised at the fervour in his blood.

It was more than simply his libido stirring. It was something new, this feeling that swelled within him.

As if sensing a change, Cassie shifted a fraction and tilted her head, trying to gauge what it was.

'What were you saying about my English class earlier? You said you wanted to talk about it.'

'Did I?' Amir stroked his index finger along the platinum chain, between her breasts to the low-cut lace of her bra.

'Amir!' He grinned, but she pulled free. 'You're incorrigible.'

'Don't you mean irresistible?'

'That too.'

For long seconds he stared into the beckoning softness of

her violet eyes. Such warmth he read there. Such happiness and admiration. It cloaked him, making him feel more like a king than at any time since his coronation. As if he was invincible.

Anyone looking at Cassie now would mistake her for a bride, just discovering passion and dreaming of love.

Amir stiffened, appalled at where his mind had wandered.

Cassie would one day marry a man of her own culture. A man who would give her everything she desired. Everything she deserved. Even love—the one thing above all else Amir could give no woman. How could he when he knew nothing of it? Love for a child, yes, he could imagine that growing as he held his babe in his hands. But love for a woman?

What were the chances he'd ever love the woman chosen to be his bride simply because she fitted his requirements for the position of queen? Instantly he rejected the idea.

Amir's hands clenched as he fought surging nausea at the idea of Cassie in love with another man. Touching another man. Even smiling at one!

Still this possessiveness lingered, growing stronger each day. Was there no cure for it?

'I said I'd heard your classes were a great success.' He forced himself to concentrate. 'You should be proud. The idea of classes on the move was an inspiration.'

'Thank you. We enjoy them.'

Amir reached out to touch the priceless sapphire, watching it quiver with every breath Cassie took. His primitive self basked in the way it marked her as *his woman* just as surely as if she still wore the slave chain.

His woman.

He'd never felt so proprietorial.

Even after all this time he was as eager for her company as ever. More so. The thought of her strong yet softly yielding body beneath him was a constant distraction as he battled to concentrate on affairs of state.

Surely the novelty must pall soon? Yet he couldn't imagine

tiring of Cassie, so intoxicatingly erotic in his arms. Nor could he imagine growing bored with her company, her quick, irreverent wit and her mulish, endearing independence. The joy of just being with Cassie.

The thought brought him up short, alarm bells ringing. It gave him the strength to say what must be said.

'You might want to consider keeping your students in the classroom for a few weeks.' A rough note edged his voice. 'Let one of the other teachers take the group around the city.'

Deep inside pain needled his belly. Guilt?

'Why? That's part of their success. It's why they work so well, and the women are enthusiastic.'

'I'm sure a lot of it is to do with you, Cassie, not just the location.' He paused, wishing he hadn't raised this. 'But Faruq tells me you're attracting a lot of attention.' He raised his hand when she made to respond. 'I know it's great publicity for the programme, but from what Faruq says it won't be long before local journalists sniff around for a profile piece.' He held her bewildered gaze. 'My staff are discreet, Cassie, but once the press gets interested they'll dig up the fact you spent a week as my sex slave.'

'I didn't!'

The jab of pain in his belly became a searing dagger-slash as he watched her bright eyes shadow. Her mouth tightened and she swallowed as if in pain.

He'd done that to her.

'You and I know the circumstances. But imagine the salacious stories once they hear you were given to me and what our accommodation consisted of.'

It would be no time at all before the press shouted what now was only whispered in inner circles: that Cassie was his lover, flaunting herself in the palace even as arrangements proceeded for a royal betrothal.

Never before had Amir installed a lover in the palace. At this delicate time especially the furore would be tremendous.

'That might be a good idea. I'll think about it.'

Amir's heart clenched as he watched pride replace pain on her face. She really was a woman in a million.

He was desperate to buy them more time.

His only hope lay in the belief that soon he would grow out of this…need for her.

One day he'd take in matrimony the woman his country expected him to wed. The woman approved by the Council of Elders, who matched every one of Amir's own criteria in a wife. The woman who would give him and his children the stability he demanded. What he needed.

If only he could imagine ever wanting her as much as he did Cassie.

'Thanks. I'll be fine from here.' Cassie closed the car door and waved to the director of the language school.

This afternoon's class had gone better than expected, given they'd stayed in the classroom. The women had been as enthusiastic as ever, and there'd been a lot of laughter as well as an encouraging amount of progress.

Yet Cassie had felt hemmed in and unsettled. Amir's comments about the press had persuaded her to stop for now the roving class that had been such a success. The small school could do with the support publicity could bring, but not the notoriety of gossip about her and Amir. Sex slave, indeed!

Distaste shivered along her spine.

That tag pushed every sensitive button she had. Not surprising since she'd grown up watching men swagger in and out of her mother's life, and how the role of kept woman had brought out a calculating, hard-heartedness in her mother Cassie aimed never to emulate.

She walked through the enormous palace gates, determined to put all that from her mind.

Normally she used another entrance, marginally less grand, on the other side of the royal complex. But she'd enjoyed the chance to chat with the director rather than sit in a silent state in the back of one of Amir's gleaming vehicles that usually delivered her to her part of the palace.

Despite the noisy enthusiasm of the classes, Cassie realised she missed the chance for a chat with another woman. Amir's employees kept a discreet distance.

She smiled and nodded to a pair of uniformed guards, and made her way up the wide steps to the entrance.

The splendour of the grand foyer stopped her in her tracks. She'd never been in this part of the palace and its magnificence took her breath away.

A towering domed ceiling of gilt and azure mosaic work drew the eye from a forest of slender supporting columns. The marble floor was inlaid in an intricate geometric design that must have taken years to complete. Tiny in the immense space were clusters of antique furniture, silk rugs and enormous jardinieres filled with exotic blooms.

An army of staff was busy under the eagle-eyed direction of the palace chamberlain.

Slowly Cassie approached, loath to ask directions of the only one of Amir's employees who'd made her feel not unwelcome but uncomfortable. His piercing grey eyes never warmed and there was a cool punctiliousness to his manner that made her wonder if he disapproved of her.

'Miss Denison.' He bowed. 'How are you?'

'Fine, thank you, Musad. And you?'

'Well, thank you.' He folded his hands, watching her with a complete lack of expression she found unnerving. 'Can I assist you?'

Cassie smiled. 'If you would. I'm afraid I'll need directions to my rooms. I'm bound to get lost from here.' The sprawling palace covered hectares.

Musad didn't smile in response, merely inclined his head. 'Of course. The way to the harem is not easy from these public areas. Deliberately so.'

'Harem?' She was staying in a *harem*? It sounded so antiquated. So *suggestive*.

Something flickered in his cool eyes. 'Yes. That is the name given to the place where the women of the King live.' He lifted his hand and one of the servants cleaning a nearby chandelier hurried towards them. 'I'll have someone show you the way.'

The women of the King. Cassie supposed that meant the monarch's female relatives, yet she couldn't banish a trickle of horror, remembering stories about concubines immured in harems for some man's pleasure. That didn't apply to her. She was Amir's guest, not his possession.

'You're having a spring clean, are you?' she asked brightly, changing the subject.

Musad nodded. 'Preparations for the forthcoming celebrations will take weeks. It's a massive undertaking.'

'What are you celebrating?'

His head jerked up as if struck, and Cassie read what looked like shock in the chamberlain's stiff features. His eyes rounded and his jaw slackened.

The servant he'd summoned stopped before them. Musad waved him abruptly away before gathering himself and wiping his face clear of expression once more.

His reaction to her question confused and disturbed. What was going on?

'Come, Miss Denison, I'll show you to your rooms myself.' He turned and gestured for her to accompany him across the vast space.

Intrigued at the change in him, Cassie followed his lead, nodding vaguely as he spoke of the dimensions of the grand hall, the age of the wall paintings and the jewels embedded in the walls, designed to glitter by lamplight and remind visitors of the royal family's immense wealth.

His patter continued as they proceeded past vast reception rooms and wide hallways, each more splendid than the last, till Cassie was filled with a numb sense of dismay at how incredibly rich Amir was.

Her lips curved in a mirthless smile. Of course he was

wealthy. She'd known it from the start. But walking endless corridors filled to the brim with treasures only reinforced the enormous gulf that existed between his world and hers.

How had she ever hoped they might—?

What? The cynical voice deep inside probed her sudden pain, like a tongue seeking out a sore tooth. *What did you hope? That he'd want more than an affair? That he'd want something long-term?*

You've fallen in love with a king, not an ordinary man.

Yet hope lingered. The fragile dreams she'd harboured refused to die.

'You never did tell me, Musad.' She broke into speech—anything to silence the knowing little voice in her head. 'What celebration is it you're preparing for?'

Musad stopped and regarded her gravely. Again she caught a flicker of something in his eyes. She would almost swear it looked like sympathy!

'A royal event,' he murmured slowly, as if reluctant to speak. Fascinated, Cassie watched him draw a deep breath. 'It will mark the formal betrothal of our Sheikh.'

'The formal…?' For the life of her Cassie couldn't force out the next word. Desperately she groped for a near pillar, clutching at it for support as her legs wobbled alarmingly.

Musad nodded. 'Our Sheikh is to marry a woman from one of the most prominent Tarakhan families.'

Dimly Cassie registered Musad's gentle tone, as if he regretted breaking the news. In slow motion she saw him raise a hand to fiddle with his perfectly arranged headcloth. Her pulse decelerated to a heavy thump and for a moment she wondered idly if she might faint as the world spun around her and nausea rose in an engulfing tide.

Amir was to marry. Betrothal celebrations were imminent. Which meant he'd been planning his wedding while keeping Cassie here as…what? His mistress?

Cassie's fragile dreams shattered in a moment that stretched out to accommodate infinite pain.

CHAPTER FOURTEEN

'FOOL, fool fool!' Cassie paced her room, allowing anger to surge, hoping it might relieve the gaping ache that filled her soul. The emptiness where hope and happiness had resided.

Amir hadn't promised for ever. He hadn't promised anything. Nor had she demanded any assurances from him. She'd told herself it was enough that they shared their bodies, shared themselves with no strings attached, because they weren't hurting anyone. That what they had was open and honest. In her innocence she'd believed their relationship was special, that eventually Amir would come to feel what she did. That at least there was a *chance*.

But there'd been nothing honest about what Amir had done. He'd kept her in his house, in his *harem*, while he arranged to marry to another woman!

Pain ripped through Cassie and her pace faltered as she doubled up, her knuckles pressed to her mouth to stop a cry of distress.

She felt…betrayed. She felt cheapened by what she'd allowed Amir to do to her.

She felt disgust, reliving the moment when as a child she'd realised what her mother did for money. Yet now it was *self*-disgust Cassie felt. Its taste was bitter gall on her tongue.

What she'd thought wondrous had merely been Amir using her to satisfy his physical needs until he settled down with his wife.

Needle-sharp pain splintered through her belly.

No wonder Musad had looked concerned. He hadn't wanted to be the one to break the news. At least he'd had the decency to take her somewhere private first.

How could she not have realised Amir played a double game?

She'd given herself to him believing they shared as equals. That this passion, this rare sense of connection, was real and worth pursuing. That he respected her as she had him. The man who'd protected her when she'd had no one else but herself to rely on. The man who'd held himself back from her, night after night, because she was so vulnerable.

His honour, his restraint, his caring had broken down the barriers she'd spent a lifetime erecting.

What had happened to that man? When had he changed?

Or had that all been a ploy to suck her into the heady spell of sensuality he wove around her?

Had he seen how needy she was for affection when she hadn't realised it herself? Had he deliberately worked on her weaknesses?

Her breath sawed as she recalled that moment today when she'd bent to pick up a pen she'd dropped in class and the women had murmured appreciatively over her new pendant as it slipped loose. One woman had claimed the blue stone was a sapphire, a rare stone of superb quality only found in a single mine in a remote part of Tarakhar. She'd claimed it was worth a fortune.

Cassie had smiled and tucked the pendant under her shirt and forgotten about it, knowing the woman was mistaken.

What if she wasn't?

Had Amir's gift been payment in kind for services rendered?

What had Cassie allowed herself to become?

She sagged against the wall, knees trembling, as the truth hit her. That necklace: the sort a rich man gave his mistress. The gossamer-fine silks and barely there underwear he provided instead of the sturdy cotton she'd once worn. The way

Amir kept her in his harem but never invited her to the other parts of the palace. He came to her bed. She'd never so much as *seen* his bedroom, and he took care to leave her before dawn each morning. He came to her at night or dusk, never in the day. Nor did he invite her to participate in any of the events he attended. She hadn't been introduced to his friends or family.

Because he was ashamed of her?

No! It was left to Cassie to feel shame.

The truth was so blindingly obvious she couldn't believe she'd never seen it. Amir didn't care enough to feel ashamed of her. He simply kept her in exquisite isolation where she could pander to his wishes and pleasure him.

Like a harem girl of old.

Bile rose in her throat but she forced it down. She had to face this.

Cassie thought of the daring way she'd caressed him with her mouth last night. She'd been so aroused by his response, revelling in the sense of power, having him so blatantly at her mercy. Now she felt sick, realising what a sham it had all been. Had he thought her enthusiasm manufactured because of his generous present?

All the time she'd given herself to him, loving him, Amir had seen her as little more than a prostitute, paying for her favours with jewellery and rich clothes and this luxurious accommodation.

No wonder he'd been so insistent she accept the pendant! It was an unspoken but necessary part of the bargain she hadn't realised she'd made.

And all that time he'd planned his future with another woman.

Air. She needed air.

Cassie stumbled to the doors that opened onto the private courtyard. As she went she scrabbled at the catch on the necklace he'd given her. The heavy stone burned like ice between her breasts, reminding her of the intimacy they'd shared and the price Amir put on it.

She yanked the chain free and flung it across the room.

Amir pushed open Cassie's door, anticipation fizzing in his veins.

He'd reorganised his schedule so he could finish early and he'd planned a surprise for Cassie: a sunset picnic at a renowned beauty spot.

He loved surprising her. The way pleasure lit her face and her eyes glowed brighter than stars. The way she turned impulsively to him, touching, talking, sharing her excitement at the smallest of things, from a moonlit swim in dark velvety water to a perfect rose.

Amir found the intimacy of that shared pleasure addictive.

Striding across the room towards the open courtyard doors, he stepped on something and frowned. It was the necklace he'd given her just last night. The gem that was such a perfect match for her lustrous eyes. Was the catch faulty? He paused to examine it but could see nothing amiss. He pocketed it and moved on.

'Cassie?'

A flash of movement caught his eye. There she was, walking in the shaded colonnade that rimmed the courtyard.

Amir stepped outside, drinking in the sight of her as a man who spied water after days in the desert. Something lifted inside him as he watched her pace quickly, all vibrant energy. She wore loose-fitting trousers that clung in all the right places and a shirt of gauzy violet that matched her eyes.

His pulse quickened.

'Cassie!'

She swung round, but instead of hurrying to meet him she stood where she was. He couldn't read her expression in the shadows but her stillness spoke of wariness, of tension.

'What's wrong?'

He covered the distance between them quickly. As he

approached she crossed her arms, accentuating the thrust of her breasts. His eyes lingered on the taut fabric even as his brain began calculating how long they could afford to linger here in pleasure without missing the spectacular sunset. They might just have time—

His eyes met hers and shock hit him.

Where was his sweet, warm lover? The engaging woman who'd stolen his attention these last two months?

Cassie's eyes flashed fire and her mouth was set mutinously.

'What's happened? Did something go wrong at school today?'

Silently she shook her head. Amir stepped forward, his hand lifting to caress her cheek.

Cassie moved back, further into the shadows.

Something slammed into him. Shock. Dismay. Why did she withdraw?

'I found this on the floor.' He dug the sapphire from his pocket and held it out.

Instead of reaching for it Cassie backed up another step, putting her hands behind her as if touching it might contaminate her. His belly tightened as something like nerves hit him. What was wrong with her?

'You can keep it. I don't want it.' Emotion vibrated in her words.

'What do you mean?' Amir paced towards her and was immeasurably relieved that she stood her ground. He wanted her close, where she belonged. 'Last night you were thrilled by it. You promised to wear it for me.'

He wanted her to wear it now. The fact that she'd dropped it on the floor sent a dart of dismay spearing through him.

'I didn't know what it was then.' Her fine brows drew together. 'It's a real gem, isn't it?'

Amir frowned at her accusing tone. 'It is. A sapphire from—'

'I don't care where it's from. I don't want it!'

'And you wonder why I didn't tell you all about it last night?' This woman drove him crazy. How many others would have leapt on the extraordinary piece just for its monetary value? He spread his hands. 'I realise you're not comfortable with expensive gifts, so I—'

'Lied.'

Amir stiffened. 'I didn't lie. I just told you it was a trinket.' That was true. With his wealth, the cost of it was trifling. 'I saw it and wanted it for you. Is that a crime?' Her attitude rankled. The way she glared up at him, as if he'd done something wrong, was ridiculous.

'I don't like being lied to.'

Angry, Amir shoved the necklace in his pocket. 'If it offends you so much I'll take it away.' What had got into her?

'I don't want *anything* from you.'

Amir frowned. 'What does it matter? I'm a rich man. It pleases me to give you pretty things.'

Her chin tilted up. 'Like it pleases you to keep me as your mistress?'

Cassie's words sent a prickle of warning down his nape.

'I wouldn't use the word *mistress*.' There'd been other women—plenty of them—he'd put in that category. But not Cassie. She was different. This wasn't a mercenary arrangement.

'What term *would* you use? Kept woman? Bit on the side?' The words snapped like staccato bites eating into his skin.

'Don't talk like that! We're lovers.'

Slowly she shook her head. 'No. Lovers share. Lovers are equals. But we're not, are we? I thought we were. But it's impossible.'

'Why?' He stepped closer still, driven by an urgency he didn't comprehend. All these weeks they *had* been equals, sharing a gift so precious he'd never experienced anything like it. He'd told himself at first it was purely sex, but denial could only last so long. This was about far more than satisfying the libido.

With Cassie he felt…

'Because you're getting married.'

The words fell like blocks of ice into a surging sea.

'Because you've made me into your prostitute, your private whore, buying my favours while you plan to marry another woman.'

Horror froze Amir as he looked into her pale, set face and read the anguish in her eyes.

'Now, stop right there! It wasn't like that.' How could she talk about herself in that way? His stomach churned in fierce denial.

'No?' One eyebrow arched in magnificent disbelief. 'What was it like, then?'

Amir's hands clenched at his sides. He smarted from the insult she offered them both.

'You know it wasn't like that. I didn't pay you. This—' his gesture encompassed the secluded garden and her private suite '—has been about us alone, no one else. What has happened between us is genuine, Cassie. I…care for you.' The words were out of his mouth without conscious decision, stunning him as he realised his feelings ran bone-deep.

For a moment she stared up with a look in her eyes that told him she wavered.

'Yet you conveniently forgot to mention you were going to marry soon. That our relationship was doomed before it started.'

Amir frowned. 'I never spoke to you of marriage. You can't have expected—'

Her bitter laugh cut him off. 'No, I couldn't have, could I? That would have been the act of a naïve fool, wouldn't it?'

Yet her voice betrayed pain as well as anger.

How could she have imagined he'd marry *her*? She was passing through, a foreigner with no lasting interest in his country. How could he marry a bride who'd been given to him as a sex slave? Who, albeit through no fault of her own, would create almost as much scandal as his own mother had when those circumstances became known? Tarakhar needed an accomplished woman of good repute as its queen. A woman who would bring his carefully nurtured plans to life.

He needed that.

Cassie and he…it was lust, desire, hunger between them. And liking. Respect too. He cared for Cassie. But that wasn't enough to build a successful royal marriage.

'You lied, Amir.' She almost spat the words and he stiffened. 'You lied by omission. You owed it to me, and to your fiancée, to tell the truth about your marriage plans.'

'She's not my fiancée.'

Cassie shook her head, fire dancing in her eyes.

Despite her accusations and the roiling mix of emotions churning inside an urgent need consumed him—to reach out and pull her close, stop her mouth with his kisses, stroke the tender skin of her throat and lose himself in shared passion. His need for her weakened him.

'Not yet. But the deal's as good as done, isn't it? Your staff know about it. How many others?'

Amir shrugged, disliking the sense of being pushed onto the back foot.

'My plans to marry don't impact on what we have. I told you I intended to wed.'

'So you did.' Her voice was saccharine sweet as she folded her arms again. 'But I thought you were talking about some day in the future. How was I to know you'd already picked a bride and made arrangements to marry her?'

'It's not relevant to us.' Desperation stirred that he couldn't make her understand. And that it mattered so much that she did.

'No?' She lunged forward and prodded him square in the chest with her index finger. 'And what about when you're married? Would it have been relevant then? Or would you have kept me on after the wedding? Does the idea of having both a wife and a concubine turn you on?'

'Don't be crude.' How could she even *think* he'd treat her that way? Nausea curled in his belly at her words.

But what was his excuse?

She'd honed in on the one flaw in his plans. For weeks he'd told himself he'd end their liaison as soon as it began to pall. That there'd be plenty of time to break it off before the wedding. That this was one final fling before he settled down to domesticity. Yet there'd been no sign of it palling. No ennui, no predictability. Instead his need for Cassie grew stronger each day.

Amir had refused to face the fact that one day soon he'd have to give her up. That this liaison which brought him such satisfaction had to end before he took his bride.

'You call *me* crude when you install me as your mistress? When you pay me in jewels and fine clothes and think that will stop me caring about the fact you're promised to someone else? When you decide I'm not good enough to meet your friends or to present in public? That I'm only good for—'

'Enough!' The roaring sound of his voice echoing through the portico shocked him. His pulse thrummed heavily, almost blotting out the sound of his laboured breathing. Fire scorched his chest and belly as he fought a turbulent tide of emotion. 'There was no insult intended, Cassie.'

She blinked, and for a moment he could have sworn he saw the glitter of tears on her lashes. The sight gutted him.

'And when you warned me off going out with my class in public?' Her voice was low now, and husky, as if her throat were tight like his. 'Tell me that was solely for my benefit. Tell me you weren't worried the publicity would interfere with your marriage arrangements.'

Guilt engulfed Amir. She was right. He'd thought of himself, smoothing things over till the time came to put Cassie away from him.

'Don't bother answering that. I can see it in your eyes. You weren't protecting me. You were protecting yourself.' She huffed out a laugh that wrenched at his heart. 'You know, I thought you different from the rest. A man of honour. A man I could respect. Naïve, wasn't I?'

The raw anguish in her husky voice pierced him and pain surged as if from a gaping wound. He reached out to her cheek. How had something so perfect gone so horribly wrong?

'*Habibti*, I—'

Cassie knocked his hand away and swung round to stare out over the darkening courtyard. But not before he'd seen tears well in her eyes. Razor-sharp talons tore at him. He'd never felt anything as intensely as this torture, watching her distress.

'I'm *not* your beloved! I may have given you my innocence but I'm not a fool. Don't insult me like one.'

Her innocence?

Amir swayed with shock. She couldn't be serious. No innocent would have blatantly seduced him the way she had, demanding he make her his. She'd been like flame in his hands, all hot energy and enthusiasm. She'd been no shrinking violet but had enjoyed sex with an honest delight that had shaken him to the core.

A delight mixed with wonder, he now remembered. And moments of hesitation that he'd convinced himself he'd imagined.

That smear of blood on the sheet! The stain that had been beneath their hips after he took her that first time. Amir recalled the ecstasy of that joining, how incredibly tight she'd felt as she gripped him and sent him over the edge.

He stared, dumbfounded, and saw the fine tremors racking her body.

What had he done?

'Cassie.' His voice was unsteady. His vocal cords paralysed. 'I didn't want it to be like this. I just wanted *you*.'

He'd thought about nothing else. For the first time he hadn't planned ahead. He'd acted on instinct, grabbing greedily at this woman and not relinquishing her. Now she was paying for his selfishness. He'd never felt so helpless in his life.

'But it *is* like this.' She sounded drained, her voice empty. 'I let you make me your mistress. I didn't even realise I was turning into the very woman I'd vowed never to become.'

Again that huff of laughter that sounded more like pain. Something twisted in his chest at her anguish.

'How's that for blind? That I of all people didn't realise what I'd become till today. That while I hoped for something else, you'd turned me into the other woman.'

'Of all people?'

She swung round, and the sight of tears trickling unheeded down her pale cheeks hit him like a sledgehammer to the solar plexus. Even in the mountains when she'd feared for her life Cassie hadn't cried.

For the first time in his memory fear overwhelmed him.

He wanted to hold her close, soothe her with gentle caresses. But the pain in her eyes, the memory of her accusations, stopped him.

Her mouth twisted in an ugly grimace. 'All my life I've fought for my self-respect. Don't think I didn't see the look in your eyes when I said I did whatever I could to make ends meet when acting jobs dried up. But I never sold myself!'

Amir opened his mouth to assure her he hadn't thought she had, but she was speaking again, her eyes glazed as if she looked inwards and didn't see him.

'I told myself I'd never be like her, and now I am, and it feels…' She shuddered and wrapped her arms around herself.

'Like whom, Cassie?' He lifted his hand to her shoulder and then dropped it, helpless in the face of her distress.

Huge bruised violet eyes lifted to his. 'My mother. I didn't tell you much about her, did I?' Her chin tilted up gallantly even as she swallowed convulsively. Pride and shame and hurt flitted across her drawn features.

'She was a rich man's mistress. She was married to someone else when she got pregnant by my father. When her husband kicked her out because he discovered the affair she moved to Melbourne and lived as my father's mistress for years. Living off his bounty and the crumbs of his attention. When he'd had enough of her she found herself another protector. Then another. One of them even decided that since he'd bought my mother he could have me too.'

Amir rocked back on his heels. At his gasp of horror her lips tilted in a vague smile.

'He didn't succeed. After that I never went home for holidays. But watching my mother prostitute herself, seeing the woman she became, I vowed never to be like her. Till you, I avoided getting close to any man.'

She shook her head, arms wrapped tight around her torso as if to hold in pain.

'And look at me now!'

Her pride, her distress, evoked a surge of emotions such as he'd never known.

Amir could stand no more. He dragged her to him, his hold careful yet unbreakable, as if he held the most fragile substance in the world. Her fragility scared him. Within the circle of his embrace Cassie stood stiff and unyielding, yet her tears wet his shirt and her gasping breath was hot against his chest.

Guilt carved a dark cavern in his soul. How had he thought himself honourable when his selfishness had wounded her so? What sort of man was he?

Never had he felt such shame and regret. Her despair and self-loathing vibrated in each word, every stifled sob. Every tremor racking her body was a blow straight to his heart. How could he ever—?

'Amir?' The tears had stopped and her voice held barely a wobble.

'Yes?' He just prevented himself adding an endearment and his hand itched to stroke her, ease her torment.

'I want to leave now. I never want to see you again.'

CHAPTER FIFTEEN

THREE weeks later Cassie looked out of the window of her rural classroom. Mountains rose in the distance. She tried not to think about that week she'd spent in Bhutran. Or about the man she'd met there. The man who'd stolen her heart when she wasn't looking and shattered it.

How could she love him still?

It was ridiculous. Pathetic.

After what he'd done to her he should mean less than nothing to her. After what she'd done to herself.

Amir wasn't solely to blame. Cassie had allowed herself to be swept on a tide of desire, enthralled by what he made her feel not just physically, but emotionally. For the first time Cassie had felt whole, content and joyously happy sharing her life with Amir.

Was this how her mother had felt all those years ago? Could it have been love after all that had driven her to follow Cassie's father and give up everything in the process?

Once, the idea had seemed preposterous, knowing the calculating, self-absorbed woman her mother had become. But now Cassie knew how devastating love could be. How dangerously strong its pull.

How could she still long for Amir's touch? How could she miss the deep rumble of his voice, or the glitter in his eyes when he teased her over a game of chess? She even missed listening to him talk about plans for urban renewal!

It scared her that, though she felt pain and shame at having allowed herself to become 'the other woman' in a relationship triangle, her main emotion was grief. Grief at the loss of Amir.

She had to get a grip!

Behind her came the sound of women's voices, her students practising in pairs the simple conversation she'd taught them. She needed to forget these daydreams and stop feeling like a victim.

Cassie moved to the nearest pair, nodding encouragement and automatically helping when the new English vocabulary eluded them.

Classes kept her sane. They gave her purpose and even a measure of happiness, seeing the difference even she, with her minimal qualifications, could make to the lives of these women. She even got to use her dramatic skills sometimes, miming concepts to help the class understand and breaking down language barriers with laughter.

She didn't miss acting as she'd thought she might. She'd even begun to think of teaching English long-term. Not here in Tarakhar. That would be prodding an open wound, knowing she was so close to Amir and his carefully chosen perfect bride.

Cassie moved between the groups, assisting when needed and praising the women who a couple of weeks ago had been too shy to speak English aloud.

How far they'd come. Their determination to improve made her ashamed of how she kept dwelling on her time with Amir rather than the future.

It didn't matter that the future was a grey, foggy place she couldn't see clearly or be enthusiastic about. She had to push herself.

The door opened and she turned to see the principal enter, excitement bright in her eyes and quick gestures.

'Ms Denison.' The principal nodded to her. 'Excuse the interruption. We have important guests, here on an impromptu visit. Such an honour!' Already she was turning to the class and addressing them in their own language.

Cassie watched as the women sat straighter, their chatter dying into a hush of expectant silence. Discreetly clothes were straightened and hair smoothed as they turned towards the door, their faces alight with excitement.

In this rural area visitors were a source of endless interest. Look at the fuss *her* presence had caused, the sole foreigner for half a day's travel.

She turned, a polite smile on her face, then froze, appalled, as her blood congealed in her veins. The words of welcome dried on her lips as she took in the tall figure in white, his stern, proud face so frighteningly familiar.

She hadn't seen Amir in weeks, yet he visited her dreams every night. She discovered she'd forgotten nothing of his austere, masculine beauty.

Just looking at him hurt as she remembered the profound joy they'd once shared.

A gasp penetrated the silence, drawing all eyes to her.

'And this is our volunteer teacher, Ms Denison.'

'Ms Denison.' He bowed, his penetrating dark gaze unreadable as it flicked her from head to toe. Instantly her body heated to tingling awareness that even shock couldn't douse. He looked so *good*, his features as magnetic as ever, though his mouth was grim and she noticed new lines bracketing his lips as if he'd given up smiling.

'Your Highness.' Her voice was husky. She was surprised to discover it worked. Her feet were rooted to the spot and her heart catapulted against her ribs as if trying to break free. A dull queasiness stirred and for one horrible moment she thought she'd be sick.

She dragged her gaze from Amir's and the unbearable tension snapped down a notch.

'Faruq.'

'Ms Denison. It's a pleasure to see you.' Faruq shook her hand and smiled as if genuinely glad to be here.

But *why* were they here? Amir was a great one for meeting his people and monitoring local issues, but she knew his life was planned to the nth degree. No spur-of-the-moment visits for him.

Unless... Could he be here to see *her*? Unbidden, the thought rose and refused to be banished. Excitement and anxiety filled her as she listened to the interchange between Amir and the suddenly shy group of women.

Tension crawled through her, tightening every nerve.

What could he want? What was there to say between them? Even here in the provinces she'd heard about the approaching betrothal celebrations and the wedding to come.

Amir had let her walk away, never attempting to detain or persuade her. Her presence in the palace was a potential embarrassment, and it was obvious nothing was more important than his carefully arranged marriage to his suitable wife.

The bottom dropped out of her stomach.

She'd had weeks to get used to the idea of him with another woman and still it made fury scream in her blood and despair weight her soul.

When would she get over him?

Cassie clenched her hands and stood still, calling on every vestige of her theatrical training to project an image of polite interest.

If he could stand being here with her, then she could do the same. He would *not* see her buckle under the weight of distress.

By the time they'd finished Cassie's knees were shaking so badly she had to grope for the wall beside her, surreptitiously propping herself up as she struggled to breathe normally through lungs cramped impossibly tight.

If only they'd leave.

At last they were moving. No, they'd paused. Through her haze of shock Cassie saw the principal's surprised stare in her direction. Then, next thing she knew, the whole class was rising and filing out through the door. Furtive glances were shot her way, but they couldn't pierce the bubble of disbelief that held her in stasis.

Faruq bowed low and followed the rest, leaving only…

Without conscious thought Cassie started forward. She couldn't stay here with Amir. She just couldn't!

Each step was an achievement on legs turned suddenly to jelly. She'd almost made it to the door when a hand shot out as if to take her arm. She shied away, banging against the wall.

'Cassie.' His voice was hoarse and low, as if stretched. She felt it in every cell. 'Don't go.'

How she'd longed to hear him say that weeks ago. Despite her outrage and hurt, she'd hoped against hope he'd stop her leaving, tell her he'd changed his mind and he wanted her as more than his mistress, that he wanted her—

'No!' She didn't know if she was shouting at him or her own vulnerable self for harbouring such foolish thoughts.

The door closed quietly, his hand spread wide to hold it shut.

She didn't have to meet his gaze to know she had no hope of leaving till Amir was ready for her to go.

'How dare you keep me here against my will? How dare you show your face here? Haven't you done enough?' Her voice cracked on the last word and her lips wobbled. 'Or are you here to send me away? Is that it?' Valiantly she tried to whip up pride to counter the traitorous weakness that undermined her. 'Is it too embarrassing having an ex-mistress in the country with your wedding so close?'

'Of course not!'

His voice was tight, as if with unspoken anger, but all she registered was that he wasn't here to exile her. How stupid and self-destructive to feel relief.

'Cassie—'

'No.' She spun away on a surge of energy. 'I don't want to hear it. There's nothing to say.' She folded shaking arms and straightened her spine, focusing on the distant view of the mountains.

'You're wrong.' His voice came from just behind her. She felt the warmth of his big frame raying out to her chilled body.

Part of her wanted to sink back against him and pretend, for a moment, that everything was as it had once been.

Except it had never been as she'd imagined. What she'd thought a glorious adventure had been a tawdry affair.

'There's a lot to say,' he murmured, his low voice insinuating itself into her blood, curling deep and powerful within her.

'How is your fiancée?' She couldn't let herself weaken.

'She's not my—'

'OK, then. Your soon-to-be fiancée?'

'She's not that either.'

His words hung in the silence. Her eyes widened. Had she heard right?

Slowly she turned. He stood, shoulders squared and jaw tight, before her. His eyes wore that shuttered look she remembered so well. The one he'd worn whenever he didn't want her to know what he was thinking.

'What are you saying?'

'The betrothal will not proceed. I will not take her as my wife.'

Cassie blinked as the walls seemed to dip and sway around her.

'Cassie!' He reached out to her and she stumbled back, coming up against a desk and leaning heavily on it.

'Are you telling the truth?' But why would he lie? Cassie held no place in his world now.

His lips thinned, but the expected flash of anger was absent. 'There will be no lies between us again, even by omission.' He lifted his hand to the back of his neck, then dropped it again in a gesture that made him look almost unsure of himself.

Cassie didn't believe that for an instant. What did he want?

'What about your wedding? Even here people are talking about it.'

'It's cancelled.' He held her eyes and heat shuddered through her.

Cassie shook her head. 'It can't be. The way Musad spoke,

it was public knowledge. You said it was expected you would marry. There were contracts being drawn up and—'

'Nevertheless, it's done.' Amir lifted his shoulders in a dismissive gesture. 'There will be restitution to her family, of course. A large restitution even though the betrothal wasn't formalised. It's over.'

At first she couldn't believe the stunning news, but there was no mistaking the grim honesty in his eyes. She felt queasy with shock.

'But what about *her*? The woman you were to marry?' Was she broken-hearted? Crazy to experience fellow feeling for a woman she'd never met, a woman she'd resented and envied.

'It was an arranged marriage, Cassie, not a love match. Another husband will be found for her.'

But not a king. Not Amir. What must she be feeling?

'The news will break publicly today.' He said it so calmly.

'But won't there be a scandal?' Cassie rubbed a finger across her forehead, as if that would help her brain chug into gear. None of this made sense. 'You said you wanted to avoid that at all costs.' It had been one of the reasons he hadn't wanted *her*. Because her past was too scandalous!

'I'll ride it out.' His look told her he had other things on his mind.

Cassie sagged lower onto the table, shaking her head.

'Don't you want to know why?' He stepped closer, and Cassie had a sense of the room crowding in around her, yet she didn't have the energy to move.

Silently she nodded. Of course she did.

'I couldn't marry her. I couldn't marry anyone, I discovered, simply for the sake of my country and because it was expected. Not even a stable, sensible partner of impeccable breeding and excellent reputation who fitted my plans exactly.'

'I don't understand. Why are you telling me this?' Disjointed thoughts tumbled through her brain, yet Cassie couldn't make sense of them.

'I couldn't marry her when it's someone else I want.'

His voice rang clear and strong, jerking her gaze up to his. He stood so close she could see the fire kindling in his dark eyes. It made her skin prickle and shrink over her bones. It made her feel...

Finally his words sank in and she shot to her feet.

'No, you can't mean—'

'I do, Cassandra.' He spoke slowly and clearly, as one might recite a vow. The idea stirred silly, vulnerable longing in her. 'I want you.'

'Well, you can't have me!' When would this torture end? She'd taken herself to the other side of the country, hoping to find some sort of equilibrium, and here he was, tempting her with some devil's bargain.

'I won't be your mistress!'

'I don't want you as my mistress.' Another pace brought them toe to toe. 'I want you as my wife.'

For a second, then another and another, she stood gawking, processing his words. Then her hands slammed into his chest and she shoved with all her might.

He didn't budge. Desperate fury rose.

'Don't you *dare* play such games with me!' Her voice was a hoarse rasp of agony.

Large hands clamped on hers, pressing them against his chest. The rapid thud of his heart pounded beneath her palm like a runaway horse.

'It's no game.' He drew in a mighty breath and her hands lifted with the movement of his torso. 'You left and nothing was the same.' His fingers tightened on hers. 'The colour leached from my world when you went, Cassie. I hadn't realised till then how much you mean to me.'

She shook her head. 'I don't want to hear this.' It had to be some sort of trick. She didn't have the strength to pick herself up a second time.

'Please hear me out.'

Cassie's eyes rounded at the desperation in his voice. She

looked up into sober eyes that shone with...*anxiety*? Was it real or did she imagine it?

'All those weeks together I told myself it was infatuation. That once lust was sated I'd move on, do my duty and marry a suitable wife. It was what I'd spent so long planning, after all. I was a coward—telling myself I acted to protect my country and my unborn children when really I hid from the possibility of true intimacy. Of caring.'

His mouth twisted grimly.

'I was thoughtless and self-absorbed. But what I felt didn't pass. I was drawn deeper. That day I urged you not to go out with the class? Yes, I wanted to avoid publicity, but it wasn't so much to protect the marriage arrangements but so I could keep you to myself for as long as possible. Because I couldn't let you go.'

Cassie's mouth dropped open, not only at his words, but at the tension in his stance, the vehemence of his tone.

'It wasn't till you confronted me that I realised what that meant.'

She licked her dry lips, watching emotions flicker across Amir's face, unable to look away.

He lifted one hand to cup her jaw, his fingers splayed over her cheek, and her eyelids fluttered at the thrill rioting through her dormant hormones.

How could his touch awaken her? She should stop him, but for the life of her she couldn't move.

'I told you that day I cared for you, Cassie. The truth is I love you.'

Her eyes blurred and heat slammed into her chest, crushing it tight as she fought to hold on to sanity. They were just words designed to tempt her. Yet she longed so much for them to be true. How could he be so cruel?

She opened her mouth to speak but nothing emerged. In that instant his head dipped low. Cassie stiffened and tried to pull back, but he held her remorselessly, ignoring her gasp of distress as he took her lips.

It was a gentle, tender caress so piercingly sweet she almost wept.

'It's not true,' she whispered when he lifted his head. Yet he surveyed her steadily, his expression unlike any she'd read before. Determined yet uncertain.

Inside her poor, bruised heart leapt.

'On my life it's true, Cassie. I was never more serious.'

Long fingers cupped her jaw, then caressed her cheek. Was that her trembling or him? Her eyes widened. The sincerity in his voice sounded real, as if it was dredged from his very soul. Was anyone that good an actor?

'I think I've loved you almost from the first,' he confided. His hand slipped gently into her hair to massage her scalp, making whorls of pleasure spiral through her. 'You were so strong, so determined, so beautiful. Your courage alone made me yearn to understand you.'

'You didn't want me for my courage.' Cassie tried to pull her defences close, still not ready to believe his easy words. 'You wanted my body.'

'Of course I did. What man wouldn't? You're beautiful, sweet Cassie.' His smile was bittersweet. 'That was the trouble, I couldn't see past that till the day you confronted me with what I'd done. I couldn't see that this wasn't simply lust. That it was much, much more.'

Staring up into his eyes, Cassie wanted to believe him so badly. Already something melted inside at the urgency of his words and the yearning in his gaze.

'Then I saw what I'd done to you.' He clasped her tight. 'Cassie, can you forgive me? I had no idea until that evening. I didn't *let* myself think about it, though Faruq and Musad tried to persuade me to break with you.'

'They did?' She'd known Musad didn't approve of her, but Faruq too?

He nodded. 'Musad fretted over the potential scandal, but Faruq feared what the situation would do to *you*. He saw what

I was too blind to see. I was too wrapped up in my own selfish pleasure to listen.'

Amir lifted her hands, pressing kisses on each.

'It wasn't love you felt. Just lust.' Desperately she tried to shore up her defences against insidious temptation. She wanted Amir's love so desperately.

'It *was* more, Cassie. But I've had a lifetime believing love doesn't exist because I'd never known it. Never seen it up close. I didn't believe it could hit me like it has. I wanted you so badly I didn't think past my needs. I wanted you happy and I let myself believe you were.'

There was anguish in his eyes and Cassie's heart lurched. A spark of warmth flared. 'I *was* happy.'

'Really?'

'Yes.' Stunned, she watched light blaze in the velvet blackness of his eyes. Could this possibly be real?

'So you…care for me?'

The uncertainty in his voice tore at her. The Amir she knew was always sure of himself. That, above all else, convinced her. She drew a shaky breath and the cramped tension in her chest eased.

'Of course I care. How could you not realise that?' Her voice was gruff.

Slowly Amir smiled. The tightness around his mouth disappeared as he grinned down at her. The warmth of that grin wrapped around her like an embrace.

'You do? Enough to forgive me?'

'I…' Cassie tried to be sensible, to remind herself of the pain he'd wrought. But suddenly being cautious didn't seem sensible—not with Amir here, looking at her as if she was the most precious thing in his world. Not when her dreams were coming true.

She swallowed hard, dredging her courage. 'I love you, Amir. I—'

The rest of her words were obliterated as his head swooped down and he took her lips in an open-mouthed kiss that tore the last shreds of thought from her. This was no tentative foray but a bold, demanding caress that heated her blood and made her shiver in delicious anticipation.

Cassie kissed him back, holding his face in her hands and tugging him lower as she stood on tiptoe, pressing herself against him with the urgency of a woman who'd found her man against all odds.

'It's not real,' she gasped when the kiss ended.

Amir tucked her close, arms wrapped tight round her. 'It's real, sweetheart. Believe it.' He drew a shuddering breath. 'I couldn't bear to lose you. I want you with me always.'

He drew back enough that she could see his face.

'Can you forgive me, Cassie?'

She saw the shadow of fear in his eyes and her heart swelled, blanking out the last of her doubts. 'Yes.'

He smiled and it was like the sun emerging from behind clouds. His hold firmed. 'Will you marry me, Cassie?'

A world of hope and love lay in those words, yet she hesitated. 'You didn't want a wife who was notorious. You wanted someone with an unblemished reputation—'

'When I lost you I got a short, sharp lesson in what *really* matters. No gossip could stop me making you mine. Besides, nothing you do could come close to the antics of my parents. They filled the tabloids for years. Yet I survived. Our children will be fine.'

For a dizzying moment Cassie's brain stuck on the notion of having children with Amir.

'But there'll be an awful fuss. The story of me being given to you will get out.'

'And we'll survive the headlines. Besides, when people come to know you it will be water under the bridge— especially when they see how devoted we are to each other.'

It sounded like heaven.

'But I'm a foreigner. I don't speak the language.'

'You're intelligent. You'll learn. The fact you've already spent time teaching here will stand you in good stead.'

'And what if it comes out who my mother was? How she lived?' She forced the words out, old shame clogging her throat. 'I can't do that to you, Amir.'

His hands tightened and his mouth turned grim. 'You are not your mother, Cassie. Any more than I am my parents. I'm tired of worrying about public opinion. My people have accepted me and they'll learn to love you too.' He stroked his palms over her face, into her hair, and held her while he pressed a gentle, loving kiss to her parted lips.

The perfection of it brought tears to her eyes. Love welled in her heart for this man who understood her so well. The one man in the world for her.

'The past is the past, sweetheart. I refuse to let it destroy what we've got. This is too precious. *You're* too precious.'

She gazed up into that beloved, familiar face, devoid now of any trace of arrogance. Instead Amir looked determined and endearingly vulnerable.

A shadow flickered across his face. 'You still haven't answered me.'

Cassie smiled, feeling the answer deep inside and knowing it was right. She let everything she felt show in her eyes. 'I'll be your wife, Amir. You're the one man in the world for me.'

Happiness and love blazed in Amir's face. The sight stole Cassie's breath.

'I couldn't ask for anything more.' He raised her hand and pressed a fervent kiss to her palm. 'Now, let's go and break the news to the crowd outside. The sooner we announce our engagement, the sooner we can be together always.'

EPILOGUE

IN THE end Amir refused to wait long for the wedding. The betrothal celebrations were barely ended when the nuptials began.

Secretly Cassie wondered if it was abstinence that motivated his desire for an early wedding. Instead of installing her in the harem on their return to the capital Amir had taken her to the house of his cousin, an academic whose claim to the throne had been bypassed when Amir had been made Sheikh.

If Cassie had had worries about jealousy between the cousins, or not being welcomed, they were dispelled within minutes of arriving. Within an hour she and Amir were the centre of an impromptu party with Amir's cousin, his wife, his wife's sister and husband, and a gaggle of excited children.

Cassie remembered what Amir had said about being isolated as a boy. But if Amir the loner felt any qualms about the lively family gathering they didn't show.

At the end of the afternoon she saw him holding the hands of a toddler while the little girl jumped up and down on his knees. The tender look in his eyes made Cassie's heart melt, especially when he looked up and held her gaze.

The world fell away and there was only them, and the promise of their future to come. It took her breath away.

It made her hope that maybe they, a pair who'd never known the love of family, would one day create their own.

For three weeks Cassie stayed with Amir's relatives, fussed over and cosseted. Finally the wedding day arrived.

That was when she truly understood how popular Amir was, how much his people wished him well. Not by a whisper or sideways glance did anyone hint at disapproval or doubt. Instead there were smiles, cheers, and an abundance of goodwill. Cassie was overcome.

There'd been speculation in the press, of course, and her story had caused a sensation in the foreign media. But instead of dwelling on titillating details most were captivated by the romance and drama of their story.

Cassie suspected Amir's masterful handling of the press had been a significant factor in the slant taken.

'Are you all right, *habibti*?' Amir's voice at her shoulder betrayed concern as they stood now before his people, receiving applause and good wishes. 'What's wrong?'

'Nothing.' She blinked rapidly. 'I'm just happy. So very happy.'

'Because of this?' He gestured to the crowd.

'That too,' she murmured, turning to face him. 'But mainly because of you.'

His eyes lit with that special fire she knew was just for her, and her heart tumbled over once more. Would she ever get used to seeing Amir's love? Hearing it in his voice? Feeling it in every touch?

Never.

He raised her hand and pressed a kiss to its centre, then turned it over and kissed her palm, lingering while his tongue swirled. She shivered with delight.

'Amir! You can't! Not in public.'

'Then we'll go somewhere private.'

'But doesn't the wedding reception have hours to go?'

He shrugged, and the devil was in his eyes. 'It does. Traditionally such occasions don't end till the early hours. But our guests will understand our absence.'

'That's what I'm afraid of.' Cassie tried to inject reproof into her voice, but instead she sounded breathless with anticipation.

'Do you mind?' Suddenly he was serious.

Cassie shook her head. 'I think it's obvious to everyone that I'm smitten.'

'That makes two of us.'

He made a deep, courtly bow, then held out his hand. Cassie placed hers in his, feeling Amir's strength, his tenderness, and knew that whatever the future held their love would last a lifetime.

Amir paused and waved to the crowd before leading her away to their private apartments.

Behind them spontaneous cheers rang out for the Sheikh and his bride.

* * * * *

Have Your Say

You've just finished your book. So what did you think?

We'd love to hear your thoughts on our 'Have your say' online panel
www.millsandboon.co.uk/haveyoursay

- 🌹 Easy to use
- 🌹 Short questionnaire
- 🌹 Chance to win Mills & Boon® goodies

Visit us Online

Tell us what you thought of this book now at
www.millsandboon.co.uk/haveyoursay

YOUR_SAY